LOOT OF THE SHANUNG

SELECTED FICTION WORKS BY L. RON HUBBARD

FANTASY

The Case of the Friendly Corpse

Death's Deputy

Fear

The Ghoul

The Indigestible Triton

Slaves of Sleep & The Masters of Sleep

Typewriter in the Sky

The Ultimate Adventure

SCIENCE FICTION

Battlefield Earth

The Conquest of Space

The End Is Not Yet

Final Blackout

The Kilkenny Cats

The Kingslayer

The Mission Earth Dekalogy*

Ole Doc Methuselah

To the Stars

ADVENTURE

The Hell Job series

WESTERN

Buckskin Brigades

Empty Saddles

Guns of Mark Jardine

Hot Lead Payoff

A full list of L. Ron Hubbard's
novellas and short stories is provided at the back.

*Dekalogy—a group of ten volumes

LOOT
OF THE
SHANUNG

Published by
Galaxy Press, LLC
7051 Hollywood Boulevard, Suite 200
Hollywood, CA 90028

Printed in the United States of America.

ISBN-10 1-59212-289-2
ISBN-13 978-1-59212-289-9

Library of Congress Control Number: 2007903619

CONTENTS

STORIES FROM PULP FICTION'S GOLDEN AGE

A ND it *was* a golden age.

The 1930s and 1940s were a vibrant, seminal time for a gigantic audience of eager readers, probably the largest per capita audience of readers in American history. The magazine racks were chock-full of publications with ragged trims, garish cover art, cheap brown pulp paper, low cover prices—and the most excitement you could hold in your hands.

"Pulp" magazines, named for their rough-cut, pulpwood paper, were a vehicle for more amazing tales than Scheherazade could have told in a million and one nights. Set apart from higher-class "slick" magazines, printed on fancy glossy paper with quality artwork and superior production values, the pulps were for the "rest of us," adventure story after adventure story for people who liked to *read*. Pulp fiction authors were no-holds-barred entertainers—real storytellers. They were more interested in a thrilling plot twist, a horrific villain or a white-knuckle adventure than they were in lavish prose or convoluted metaphors.

The sheer volume of tales released during this wondrous golden age remains unmatched in any other period of literary history—hundreds of thousands of published stories in over nine hundred different magazines. Some titles lasted only an issue or two; many magazines succumbed to paper shortages during World War II, while others endured for decades yet. Pulp fiction remains as a treasure trove of stories you can read, stories you can love, stories you can remember. The stories were driven by plot and character, with grand heroes, terrible villains, beautiful damsels (often in distress), diabolical plots, amazing places, breathless romances. The readers wanted to be taken beyond the mundane, to live adventures far removed from their ordinary lives—and the pulps rarely failed to deliver.

In that regard, pulp fiction stands in the tradition of all memorable literature. For as history has shown, good stories are much more than fancy prose. William Shakespeare, Charles Dickens, Jules Verne, Alexandre Dumas—many of the greatest literary figures wrote their fiction for the readers, not simply literary colleagues and academic admirers. And writers for pulp magazines were no exception. These publications reached an audience that dwarfed the circulations of today's short story magazines. Issues of the pulps were scooped up and read by over thirty million avid readers each month.

Because pulp fiction writers were often paid no more than a cent a word, they had to become prolific or starve. They also had to write aggressively. As Richard Kyle, publisher and editor of *Argosy*, the first and most long-lived of the pulps, so pointedly explained: "The pulp magazine writers, the best of them, worked for markets that did not write for critics or attempt to satisfy timid advertisers. Not having to answer to anyone other than their readers, they wrote about human beings on the edges of the unknown, in those new lands the future would explore. They wrote for what we would become, not for what we had already been."

Some of the more lasting names that graced the pulps include H. P. Lovecraft, Edgar Rice Burroughs, Robert E. Howard, Max Brand, Louis L'Amour, Elmore Leonard, Dashiell Hammett, Raymond Chandler, Erle Stanley Gardner, John D. MacDonald, Ray Bradbury, Isaac Asimov, Robert Heinlein—and, of course, L. Ron Hubbard.

In a word, he was among the most prolific and popular writers of the era. He was also the most enduring—hence this series—and certainly among the most legendary. It all began only months after he first tried his hand at fiction, with L. Ron Hubbard tales appearing in *Thrilling Adventures*, *Argosy*, *Five-Novels Monthly*, *Detective Fiction Weekly*, *Top-Notch*, *Texas Ranger*, *War Birds*, *Western Stories*, even *Romantic Range*. He could write on any subject, in any genre, from jungle explorers to deep-sea divers, from G-men and gangsters, cowboys and flying aces to mountain climbers, hard-boiled detectives and spies. But he really began to shine when he turned his talent to science fiction and fantasy of which he authored nearly fifty novels or novelettes to forever change the shape of those genres.

Following in the tradition of such famed authors as Herman Melville, Mark Twain, Jack London and Ernest Hemingway, Ron Hubbard actually lived adventures that his own characters would have admired—as an ethnologist among primitive tribes, as prospector and engineer in hostile climes, as a captain of vessels on four oceans. He even wrote a series of articles for *Argosy*, called "Hell Job," in which he lived and told of the most dangerous professions a man could put his hand to.

Finally, and just for good measure, he was also an accomplished photographer, artist, filmmaker, musician and educator. But he was first and foremost a *writer*, and that's the L. Ron Hubbard we come to know through the pages of this volume.

This library of Stories from the Golden Age presents the best of L. Ron Hubbard's fiction from the heyday of storytelling, the Golden Age of the pulp magazines. In these eighty volumes, readers are treated to a full banquet of 153 stories, a kaleidoscope of tales representing every imaginable genre: science fiction, fantasy, western, mystery, thriller, horror, even romance—action of all kinds and in all places.

Because the pulps themselves were printed on such inexpensive paper with high acid content, issues were not meant to endure. As the years go by, the original issues of every pulp from *Argosy* through *Zeppelin Stories* continue crumbling into brittle, brown dust. This library preserves the L. Ron Hubbard tales from that era, presented with a distinctive look that brings back the nostalgic flavor of those times.

L. Ron Hubbard's Stories from the Golden Age has something for every taste, every reader. These tales will return you to a time when fiction was good clean entertainment and the most fun a kid could have on a rainy afternoon or the best thing an adult could enjoy after a long day at work.

Pick up a volume, and remember what reading is supposed to be all about. Remember curling up with a *great story.*

—Kevin J. Anderson

KEVIN J. ANDERSON *is the author of more than ninety critically acclaimed works of speculative fiction, including The Saga of Seven Suns, the continuation of the Dune Chronicles with Brian Herbert, and his* New York Times *bestselling novelization of L. Ron Hubbard's* Ai! Pedrito!

LOOT OF THE SHANUNG

CHAPTER ONE

BILLIONS AT STAKE

THE press releases flowed across the desk in a miniature Yangtze at flood time. The office of the *Oriental Press* throbbed with effort and excitement.

Jimmy Vance, both hands full and a pencil between his teeth, stared up at the copy boy. "Here y'are. Tell them to run this on the first page. I'll hand the fills over in a few minutes. About his life and all."

"A lady to see you, Jimmy," said the copy boy.

"The devil with that. Where'd I put that *Who's Who*?"

The *Who's Who* came to light when it was going down for the third time in the tan copy paper. Jimmy flipped it open, swept his very blond hair out of his eyes, and ran his finger down the column.

"George Harley Rockham," said the *Who's Who*. "Born 1890 in Chicago, Ill. Appointed to Russian Wheat Commission, 1919. Served as Secretary of Interior, 1924–6. Held oil leases in Regular Oil Company. Developed vast holdings in South America. Created an oil monopoly in China, 1928. Known best through his hobby of travel. Married Virginia Courtney in 1908. His daughter, Miss Virginia Rockham, has long been known to Long Island Society. . . ."

"Huh," said Jimmy, "that's plenty. Plenty." He grabbed at his battered typewriter, inserted half a dozen sheets after the custom of copywriters and began to hammer the keys in an industrious hunt-and-punch system.

The copy boy, bucktoothed and mostly grin, was at his elbow again. "Jimmy. That dame says she won't wait. You got to see her. Here's the card."

"Busy," said Jimmy, continuing to write.

"She's a swell looker," informed the copy boy. "Real class."

"Beat it," said Jimmy, scowling at the *Who's Who*.

His story grew out of the roller:

> Shanghai, China, May 14, *Oriental Press*. As the fate of George Harley Rockham, the great oil magnate, tonight remained shrouded with mystery, his many friends over the world watched anxiously for the first news.

Jimmy scratched his head, scowled at the sheet and then wrote:

> It is debated that he still lives. The coastal steamer *Shanung* has not appeared in Hong Kong, and while there are no storms recorded north of that city, it is thought that the *Shanung* might have foundered, run aground or met any other perils of the sea.
>
> Rumor is current that the *Shanung* was captured by the notorious pirates who range along Bias Bay, a few miles north of Hong Kong. This is only one of many conjectures that . . .

The copy boy was there again, still grinning. "That dame gave me a five-spot to see you, Jimmy. Y'can't let me down now. I need five Mex and if you don't see her I'll have to give it back."

"Scram," said Jimmy, pondering anew. He was about to consult the *Who's Who* for further rumors, conjectures and so on when he became aware of a pair of hands on the railing before his desk.

He stopped, looking absently at the fingers. They were nice hands. White and graceful, with long, naturally polished nails. A diamond ring glittered, but it wasn't on the engagement finger.

Jimmy was suddenly interested. He looked up the arms and discovered a Cossack jacket with silver cartridge cases. He looked at the high Russian collar and then saw the face.

The face, decided Jimmy, was very pleasing. The girl's eyes were dark, rather wistful and sad. Her cheekbones were high, giving an air of severity to the features. But the fullness of the good-natured mouth belied that.

"You're Jimmy Vance?" said the girl, very quietly.

"Yes," said Jimmy and then instantly recovered himself. "If you're looking for the society editor, he's first corridor to your right." He turned back to his work, not meaning to be rude, but aware of the necessity of stopping the study of the girl.

He was about to write another paragraph on the story when he saw the card the boy had laid beside his typewriter. The card was simply engraved. It said, "Virginia Rockham."

Jimmy's eyes flashed up. It was one of the few times in Jimmy's headlong career that he registered surprise. He jumped to his feet and swung the gate back.

"Good golly, Miss Rockham. I'm sorry as the devil. I thought you must be one of these Ruskies, the way you're dressed. I didn't have any idea . . . Here, have a chair. Now listen, Miss Rockham, I've got to have some dope here before I can go on."

She was mildly surprised at his manner. Jimmy usually gave the impression of a meteor in full flight. He was not so very tall and he seemed utterly without color. His eyes were big and swift and frank. He had the air of hurrying even when sitting still. Restlessly, he offered her a cigarette and then lit one for himself when she refused.

"Dope, Miss Rockham. The presses are grinding, the boys are waiting on the streets. The international cables are holding down their keys, waiting for this stuff. I've heard opinions, I've heard theories, and now, by golly, I want to hear some facts."

"I . . . I don't know any more than you do, Mr. Vance."

"The hell you don't!" Jimmy was plainly aghast. "Well . . . well . . . think of something, anything. I've written columns on it already and I've had to make up each and every word. Good God, Miss Rockham, a billionaire doesn't disappear like that. Even out here in China. He has to be *someplace*. Even a Chinese pirate would know how much he was worth in ransom. Think, girl!"

She was studying Jimmy, listening to his voice rather than his words. Her dark eyes were suddenly alight. She sat forward.

"You're *the* Jimmy Vance, aren't you?" she said.

He was thrown into no little confusion, but he recovered quickly. "What do you mean by that?"

"You're the man who makes news news, aren't you? The

star reporter of the *Oriental Press,* the bearder of warlords and the formulator of international opinions."

Jimmy gaped at her. "Gee whiz, Miss Rockham . . . I . . . Somebody has been feeding you a line. Look here, Miss Rockham, I got to have something for the presses, the cables. I got to have *fact,* not fancy. What happened to your father?"

"He was on the SS *Shanung.* The *Shanung* isn't reported. That's all I know."

"But look here. I mean what's the well-known lowdown? What's he tied up with? Who's trying to get him? What's hanging over his head?"

"I thought . . . thought you'd know something about it," she replied.

"Me? Why should I know anything? I'm just a dumb reporter, Miss Rockham. I admit I've had a few breaks, but does that make a clairvoyant out of me? Hell, no. I mean to say, I don't know anything and I'm writing guesses."

"This is big news, isn't it?"

"Big news? Gee whiz, Miss Rockham, I'll say it is. Might as well have the president of the United States disappear as George Harley Rockham. He's got China oil in his palm. He owns more men and more companies than a nation. What made him disappear?"

"He went down to Hong Kong to look over some interests there. That's all I know."

Jimmy leaned tensely over his typewriter. "Where was he before that?"

"Chinwangtao."

7

"Up next to Manchukuo, right? What's he own in Manchukuo?"

"I'm not certain."

Jimmy smiled a swift smile. "Then he *does* own something. Why did—?"

"Wait, Mr. Vance. We're wasting time here. I came up for just one reason. I came here to see Jimmy Vance to offer him a job. I've been told and I know for myself that if anyone can find George Harley Rockham and do the job quickly, it would be Jimmy Vance. Speed is your name."

"Why speed?"

The girl's voice was low and earnest, "Because Rockham isn't as steady as a rock the way the advertisements read. He holds his industrial empire together with one finger, but when that finger slips . . ." She reached into her handbag and threw a cable report of stocks on Wall Street on Jimmy's typewriter keys.

"See those stocks?" she said, tensely. "They've lost points! And Rockham isn't here. Because he's gone, they're selling him out. If we don't find him in four days and tell the world he's safe, George Harley Rockham will be on the relief rolls. That's not for publication, Mr. Vance. That's truth. We've *got* to find him!"

"Gee whiz," said Jimmy, studying the report. "This *is* bad, isn't it?"

"I have money in my own right but it's tied up with the Rockham interests. I'd have to offer you a gamble. If you find him, you get one hundred thousand dollars. If you don't, you get nothing because there won't be anything to pay you with. Your time is valuable, but I can't guarantee a salary or anything of the sort. I have enough cash for expenses, but . . ."

Jimmy was bouncing the hook on the phone. "Gimme Bruce Conway. That's right. . . . Hello, Bruce. Listen, I'm going out to find Rockham. . . . No, I'm not nuts. His girl just came in. . . . I know it's only twenty feet to your office. . . . I haven't got time. . . . Put somebody on this desk." He hung up.

Grabbing a battered gray felt hat from its hook he snapped it down over one eye and held open the gate. "Come on, daylight's burning."

"Then . . . then you'll go?"

"Well, what the hell do *you* think?" He thrust her through the outer doors and stopped. "Look. You go to your hotel for your toothbrush. I'll charter a seaplane and get a couple of gats. Where do I meet you in a half-hour?"

"At the Palace Hotel," she said.

Jimmy vanished from sight, shouldering his way between two very large men whose heavy faces bore a mark of stolid satisfaction. Their eyes were on the girl's back as she walked away. They followed her swiftly.

Presently one of them fell into step at her side. "Pardon me, Miss Rockham, but my name's Pete Gar. This other guy is my pal Joe."

Fear flashed across her face.

"Joe's got a gun in his hand," said Pete. "So you just walk along nice and quiet or I guess we'll have to plug you."

Joe nodded in solid agreement and lifted his hand inside his coat pocket. Joe's black-bead eyes were very attentive.

9

CHAPTER TWO

"WE WANT HIM DEAD!"

JIMMY VANCE descended upon the lobby of the Palace Hotel with a very brisk stride. His eyes were feverishly alight. He shoved his gray felt hat to the back of his head, planted his arms on the desk and looked at the silk-haired, frock-coated clerk.

"Get me Miss Rockham," he ordered.

"Miss Rockham hasn't come in from a walk," replied the clerk.

"Are you sure?"

"I've been here all the time."

"Just like a woman to be late," muttered Jimmy. He paced restlessly up and down before the desk and then said, "I'll wait for her here in the lobby."

He went out into the sea of faces and soft carpets and leaned against a pillar, watching both the grillroom and the front entrance. It was nearly time for tiffin, but Jimmy did not want to spare the time to eat. Certainly, the girl would be there in a moment.

He glanced at his wristwatch on the average of every five seconds. The hands crawled slowly and certainly until an hour had passed. Jimmy stamped about the pillar and leaned against it again.

A saffron-faced, shock-haired gentleman in a morning

coat, striped pants and spats approached Jimmy. He flapped his gloves, adjusted the gardenia in his buttonhole and cleared his throat.

Jimmy whirled as though the cough had been a shot.

Cheng bowed a short bow, smiling. "Thank you, how are you?"

Jimmy knew the man fairly well. Cheng was some kind of ambassador-at-large from Manchukuo. God knew the number of mixed races which made up his ancestry.

Cheng bowed again, fumbling with his silk hat. "I see you are very worried, Mr. Vance, yes?"

"No," said Jimmy. "I'm never worried about anything except international affairs, accidents, births and deaths and lovelorn letters. Cheng, never be a newspaperman."

"No?"

"No! You'll avoid gray hairs, high blood pressure and fallen arches. Where in the name of the Almighty is that girl?"

"Perhaps I can help you," said Cheng. "What girl?"

"Miss Rockham," replied Jimmy.

"Why, she went up just a little while ago. I saw her enter the lift. One does not miss such beauty in this desolate city."

Jimmy muttered a tight thanks and strode to the desk. He confronted the clerk with an extended jaw. "What's the big idea? I thought you'd tell me when Miss Rockham came in!"

"But . . . but I haven't seen her!" protested the clerk in all his humility.

"Call her room. Have the girl call it. Do something. Daylight's burning!"

The Chinese girl at the switchboard plugged in. Jimmy saw her mouth move, saw her take the plug out. Then she nodded.

"Missee Rockham in," she said.

"What room?" demanded Jimmy.

"Five-thirteen," said the clerk, hastily.

Jimmy elbowed his way to the lift, thrust the blue-gowned boy in ahead of him and slammed the door himself. "Five!"

The elevator shot up. Jimmy strode out on the fifth floor, scanning the rooms for number 513. Then he saw that a suite bore that number. His knuckles were loud on the door.

The knob turned and drew inward. Jimmy took a step forward. Instantly a large hand was on his shoulder. He was catapulted across the rug. The door slammed solidly behind him.

Picking himself up, Jimmy turned about, his mouth twisted down, his eyes angry. "What's the big idea?"

Pete Gar juggled a .38 Colt automatic. He looked at it and then at Jimmy. "Sit down, newsy."

"Sit down yourself," snapped Jimmy. "I'm not tired. Where's Miss Rockham?"

Pete Gar pointed through another door. In this room Virginia Rockham was seated. She was gagged and her ankles and arms were lashed to the chair. Her eyes were scared and appealing.

"What's the idea?" thundered Jimmy. "You got any sense at all?"

Joe looked around the corner. His face was utterly relaxed,

13

but even then it was terrifying. His blue, unshaven jowl gave him the appearance of an ape.

"If you mean me," said Joe, "I resent that."

"Yeah, I mean you, funny-face. What's this? The well-known gag? What do you guys want?"

Pete lounged across the room, grinning. "I want you to call up for us. Otherwise, we plug the lady in there, or maybe slice on her a little."

"Call up who?" demanded Jimmy.

"Your office. You tell them George Harley Rockham is dead. Tell them you got the straight dope. They'll believe you." Pete spun the gun by its trigger guard. "You're sweet on this dame, and if you want to save her life, there's the phone."

"Nuts," said Jimmy. "Every cop in Shanghai would be on your trail in an hour."

"That's our lookout." Pete went to the window and looked down the Bund. A seaplane was tossing on the swelling Huangpu. "We'll just hop your crate and scram. It's as easy as that."

Jimmy had never waited to make a decision. He did not wait now. He strode across to the phone and picked it up, deftly tossing the receiver off the hook and catching it in his left hand. The girl's eyes were suddenly filled with terror.

Jimmy gave the number of the *Oriental Press*. Then he waited and gave a branch number.

"Make sure that's the city desk," rapped Pete, spinning the automatic.

"I know you aren't anybody's sap," replied Jimmy, almost

smiling. He tapped his foot as he waited, looking out of the window toward the seaplane which he had ordered to stand by for him.

A voice grated at the other end of the line. Jimmy promptly said, "Hello, Conway? Yeah, this is Jimmy Vance. Yeah. . . . Listen, I just got it straight. I've got conclusive proof that old Rockham's pushing up daisies. Yeah, dead. . . . Naw. I know what I'm talking about. All the rest of this is a wild goose chase, see? No need of going anyplace. He's been killed by pirates at Bias Bay. They didn't know who he was and the Navy got after them and they killed their captives. . . ."

"Sure, straight stuff. Okay, Conway, I'll be seeing you."

The voice at the other end of the wire chattered, "No blong, no blong! Thisee printee shop. No catchum nothin'. No saveee!"

Jimmy hung up with a confident smile. "Okay, boys, that's that. I've tossed away the rep for the girl. Now let her loose."

"Yeah?" said Pete. "That's what you think. Sit down in that chair there so you can watch us shove off in your crate."

Jimmy laughed. "You're too late. It's already gone."

Pete stepped quickly to the window with a hair-curling curse. He studied the face of the river. Sampans and junks were swarming there and, as a matter of fact, the plane was momentarily hidden.

"It's gone!" wailed Joe, rushing to the window.

Pete slapped the curtains aside, flattening his nose against the glass.

Jimmy jumped into the center of the room. A chair leaped

upward in his hands. Both Pete and Joe whirled, but the big chair was already coming down in a swift arc. It crashed across thick heads, splinters flying in every direction.

Joe swore and sprang to one side, not fairly hit. Jimmy swung again and what remained of the chair opened a wide gash on Joe's flat forehead.

The two wilted down, almost together. Jimmy's hands went swiftly to work. He unlashed Virginia Rockham and helped her stand.

"The plane?" she said.

"It's still there. Get what cash you have here and what you'll need. Quick!"

"But the death report!"

"I called the printery and they don't speak much English."

*Joe swore and sprang to one side, not fairly hit. Jimmy swung
again and what remained of the chair opened a
wide gash on Joe's flat forehead.*

CHAPTER THREE

A Cargo of Dead Men

AT the customs jetty down the Bund they found a sampan. The plane was visible on the yellow water, lying out of shipping's way across the stream.

The sweating coolie thrust his frail craft away from the bobbing float and they were immediately caught up by the swift current of the river.

Junks sped by, their gigantic sculling oars worked by women, their painted bow eyes headed for the sea. The sails flapped in the calm of the day, the bamboo ribs rattling against the brown burlap like skeletons' bones.

The sampan drew in beside the plane and was made fast to a float. Jimmy flung himself over the wing and reached back for Virginia Rockham. When she was safely aboard, he threw a coin to the coolie and opened the cabin door.

An impassive gentleman was sitting behind the controls, not bothering to help them in. He gazed searchingly at Jimmy and then turned back to his panel.

Jimmy studied the man. "Who the hell are you? I wanted Grogan to pilot me."

"Grogan's sick. I'm taking his place." The voice was very weary and lackluster. "Call me Burt. Where was it you wanted to go?"

The question had been in Jimmy's mind. He was not quite

certain of their destination himself. But he answered promptly, "Bias Bay or thereabouts. Shove off, pilot."

The sampan was away. The man called Burt shot the throttles all the way up. The twin engines roared, their powerful voices considerably diminished by the sound insulation of the well-appointed cabin.

The plane shot forward, heading up the river. The pilot flippered to avoid junks and ships, and then, seeing a clear stretch before them, he boosted the plane away from the water.

The hull pulled free, dripping yellow rivulets. They headed south and west, toward Bias Bay.

"Here we go," said Jimmy. "Where's the shortwave set I asked for?"

"Didn't have time to install it," said Burt, unperturbed.

"That's a hell of a note. I've got to get in touch with my paper."

"I can't help that," replied Burt.

"Cooperative, isn't he?" said Virginia. "Have you any definite plans?"

"Nope," said Jimmy with a quick smile. "Nary a plan. But the well-known old girl Miss Fortune will undoubtedly lead our footsteps. I shoulda bumped those two mugs back at the Palace." He looked disappointed and gloomy for a moment and then brightened. His expressions and moods rarely stayed constant for more than five minutes at a time.

Shanghai fled away to the north. In a surprisingly short time they picked up the coastline, following it. Ships were visible on the horizon, sometimes little more than puffs of greasy smoke.

It gave Virginia a feeling of power. She could see every one of those vessels but the vessels couldn't see each other. It was clear and had she tried, she could have computed their visible territory as stretching for a thousand square miles.

"How fast are we traveling?" she asked.

"What you logging?" Jimmy asked Burt.

"Figure it out for yourself. I'm busy." Burt's head was bent over his controls, and though his voice had had an edge, it did not show on his face.

Jimmy lifted his eyebrows in exaggerated shock, and peered at the panel himself. "Hundred and seventy-five. This baby really steps out, doesn't it?"

"When will we get there?" asked Virginia.

"In about five hours, I guess. Before dark anyway. We'll spot some small town and then everything will be fine. I'll get the local cops to help and we'll find your dad long before those four days are up."

"I hope so," replied Virginia.

Jimmy leaned back and noticed that her profile was very lovely against the metallic blue sky. She had a somewhat impertinent nose, come to think of it, and her chin was very, very firm.

He removed his hat, smoothed out his bleached hair and gave himself over to thought. Bias Bay had been a guess. But then that's where the pirates hung out and ships don't go bye-bye in calm weather unless pirates have something to do with it one way or another.

What a scoop if he found George Harley Rockham! A

21

byline on every front page in the world. Exclusive rights. The *Oriental Press* would certainly up in prestige.

Suddenly he recalled Virginia's offer of a hundred thousand dollars. He hadn't thought of it before. At the time it had merely showed him that she was in earnest about the thing.

"Say, about that hundred grand, Miss Rockham . . ."

"What about it?"

"I'm not going to take it. I'm no man hunter by trade. I'm a newspaperman."

"But you haven't even a faint idea of where Dad is, yet. Decide about it later."

"No," said Jimmy, very serious, "I'm not going to take it. I'll find him all right, never fear. But all I want is the exclusive rights to the story. The story's the thing, you know."

"You'd go any lengths to get a real dyed-in-the-wool scoop, wouldn't you."

"Sure I would. In these days of radio and newsreels and all, a scoop isn't hitting you in the face every day."

"But," said Virginia, "you won't stand to gain anything by this just writing it up. You'd have to hand it all to the *Oriental Press*."

"The story's the thing," he persisted.

"But why? What's so fine about a story? You can't eat it, you know."

Jimmy shrugged. He wasn't bothered with the task of trying to analyze just why a story was so important. It had never occurred to him that a story wasn't important, and that was that.

He dozed after a little, his head back, his eyes closed, the throb of the engines lulling him. Suddenly he felt Virginia's hand on his shoulder and sat up straight. He was aware of a change in the engines. The horizon was at a crazy angle. They were going down.

Jimmy glanced through the window and saw a ship. He could make out a dim haze of a shoreline, indistinct in the evening haze.

"Is this Bias Bay?" said Jimmy.

"Well, what do you think?" snapped Burt.

"What you landing out here for?" demanded Jimmy.

"To pick up my bearings from that ship. It's calm, or have you gone stone-blind?" Burt cut his throttles back a notch. The seaplane rocked level and streaked along the crests of the waves.

Jimmy eyed the ship ahead of them. It did not seem to have any steerageway, nor could he make out anyone on the rails. The vessel had a heavy list, had a sort of abandoned look about her.

The plane hit, bouncing from crest to crest, settling gradually. Burt thrust his right rudder into the floor and the ship coasted swiftly toward a gangway which dangled, unattended, from the steamer's rail.

When they had come to a stop, Jimmy opened the door, dropped down on the forward part of the hull and held them in close to the gangway. An instant later, Virginia was at his side.

"It's the *Shanung*!" cried Virginia, excitedly.

Jimmy looked blank for a moment and then saw the name on a life preserver which had been yanked half off its cleats.

Jimmy forgot about holding the plane in to the gangway. He jumped down on the stage and started up to the deck, Virginia close behind him.

The ship had a deserted air about her. No one hailed them. Suddenly Jimmy thrust his hands out and placed Virginia behind him.

A man, dead many days, was sprawled on the steel deck, his slanted eyes staring at the evening sky. Another was huddled in the scuppers, a blue hole in his cheek.

But he had not prevented Virginia from seeing them. She bit at her lower lip and backed toward the ladder as though anxious to escape.

"It's the ship your dad was on, all right," said Jimmy, anxious to get her mind off the dead men. "And it looks like the pirates fixed her up right. If that's the case, then your dad's been taken ashore to their hangout and we'll have to go there. No use looking over this hulk. Let's go."

He guided her to the ladder and started down. He was five steps from the bottom, so deep was his preoccupation, before he noticed the absence of the plane.

The plane was floating better than a hundred yards away, drifting in the wind. Even as he looked, Jimmy saw Burt's arm go up in a sarcastic salute.

The engines roared, the ship picked up speed, lifted, and bored air into the east.

Jimmy watched it and then gave vent to his wrath. His

eyes were spinning with the intensity of his fury and it was not until he had loosed three of the seven great sea oaths that he remembered Virginia.

Virginia looked politely shocked, determined to make the best of it. "Go on," she said, "I wish I knew some of them."

CHAPTER FOUR

MAROONED ON THE ABANDONED SHANUNG

JIMMY guided Virginia back up the ladder, hurried her across the deck toward a corner cabin, anxious to get her out of sight while he tidied up the ship.

He flung back the door and instantly recoiled. A dead man was sprawled across the rug, a dried pool of black about his shoulders.

Jimmy went to the next cabin. Virginia's eyes were wide and her mouth was set. This stateroom had not been occupied. Gladly, she went in and sat down weakly upon the leather transom.

"You stay there, Miss Rockham," ordered Jimmy. "This ship isn't fit for a lady anyhow."

"What are you going to do?"

"Oh," he said airily, "give it the well-known once-over. Ought to be some kind of evidence scattered about."

He went back to the deck and stood with his hands in his coat pockets, looking at the grisly carnage. Swallowing hard and trying to hold his breath, he approached the man in the scuppers. He turned his head aside as he lifted the thing and made a wry face.

A dead-sounding splash came back to him and he went to the next. This man had probably been an officer aboard the *Shanung*. Jimmy took hold of his sleeve and towed the queerly leaden body to the rail and pitched it through.

From the foredeck, he went aft, stopping often, feeling more than a little sick. He cleared the decks with a deliberateness one would never have suspected of him.

It was dark when he had finished. A cool drizzle came out of the murky sky, bathing the stained planking, clearing the night.

The dead ship bobbed in the slow swell, creaking and moaning as her rigging shifted. Jimmy was suddenly possessed with the erroneous idea that someone was behind him. In spite of himself, he repeatedly whirled about on his way forward.

He felt like a kid in a haunted house. There were no lights and the rain cut off the stars. He could not bring himself to walk solidly. He went as silent as a shadow to the forecastle head.

A winch was there and the anchor chains glistened dully. He knew that a sudden wind might throw them inshore and if he stayed in one place, then the chances were that he would be located.

He found the slippery release lever and yanked it. With a clattering roar the anchor went down into the sea. Wet rust flakes geysered up and Jimmy spit them out. Suddenly he was aware of another person beside him.

Whirling, hands diving to the guns in his belt, he stood paralyzed for a full ten seconds. Then he recognized Virginia.

"What's wrong?" she whispered.

"I just anchored us," replied Jimmy. He was aware of her

shaking hand. Poor kid. If the ship was getting him, what was it doing to her? "I didn't want us to drift ashore."

"Oh." She looked over her shoulder. "It was so dark back there. Aren't . . . aren't there any lights?"

"The generators aren't turning, of course," said Jimmy. "But let's go up to the bridge and see if we can't find a flash or maybe some lanterns."

Together they climbed the bridge ladder. The place was deserted. The wind whipped the canvas dodger and the slow rivulets of rain whispered in the dark.

Jimmy fumbled through lockers, his hands snarling in signal flags, and found nothing. He searched the captain's quarters without discovering anything.

Trying to make his voice sound hearty, he said, "Must be lights aboard here, someplace." He paused in thought and then snapped his fingers. Virginia jumped at the sound.

Jimmy went to the bridge wings and fumbled over the side. In a moment he returned with the red port lantern—a mammoth brass thing used in emergencies when the main running lights failed. From the starboard side he took a green duplicate and then, fumbling in his pockets for a match, he knelt beside them.

Presently the greenish light was blending with the red. He handed the port lantern to Virginia, and though it was heavy, she took the cleat in both hands, holding it as though afraid it would leap away from her.

They started to go back down the ladder. Virginia was holding back and before he reached the bottom, Jimmy stopped and returned.

"God, but it's dark down there," said Jimmy.

"I . . . I thought so, too."

"The captain's cabin is in pretty fair shape. Let's go in there." Jimmy led the way, entered and placed his lamp on the table.

He whipped the clinging drops from his jacket and turned to find that Virginia was industriously bolting the door. When that was done she went to the ports and securely battened them. This cut off the cool stream of air which had been passing through, and the cabin was instantly muggy, but it also cut off the sounds of the night outside.

Jimmy seated himself and lit one of the captain's cigars. "Funny, the way Burt put us down here."

"I was thinking about that, too."

"He must have known exactly where this ship was located in Bias Bay." Jimmy took a long drag on the cigar. The glowing end was white in the red light of the port lantern. "In fact I think those guys didn't intend to slip up. They had a connection out at the airport and made the best of it. Then they knew that if we got away from them, Burt could take care of us. But if they got us dead to rights, then Burt could be trusted to pilot them where they wanted to go."

"That sounds logical," replied Virginia. "But why should they be so anxious to have it known that Dad is dead?"

"That means your dad isn't dead."

Virginia sat up straight and her eyes took on a lively glow. "You think so?"

"I know it. If he was dead, they'd have his corpse discovered and that would be that. But if he's still alive, then they're either unable to kill him or want the rumor confirmed."

"Wait, I just happened to think—Jimmy. Pete Gar and Joe know where we are. So does Burt, naturally. Then the fellow at the bottom of all this knows where we are and intends to keep us handy for future reference."

"Meaning they're liable to be with us at any moment and God help us. Forget it and think of something nice."

Jimmy scowled thoughtfully at the red eye before him. He was wondering what he would do if Pete Gar came back with a mob to wipe him out. Now that he had his finger in it and could squawk to the cops, Pete wasn't liable to let him live so very long. And if the mob couldn't actually put their hands on George Harley Rockham, they would certainly have a use for Virginia.

"Those stocks and holdings," said Jimmy, "are the basis of all this some way. Think they'll hold us for a week?"

"Better revise it to four days," said Virginia.

Jimmy thought that over and then said, "Well, we'll give it the well-known all, anyway. We'll find some way out. I've never been stuck yet."

Virginia nodded. She seated herself on the edge of the bunk, leaning back against the wall. For minutes she watched Jimmy and then her head began to droop. Each time she brought it quickly up and sat very straight with immense concentration.

Jimmy watched her, smiling. Soon she no longer lifted her head and it lolled to one side, for all the world like a French doll's. Very silently, Jimmy crossed the room. Placing his arm across her shoulders, he eased her down to the pillow. He took off her small slippers and straightened her out.

Standing back he smiled again. The poor kid was all tired out. But she was game. Had more nerve than any other girl he had ever known. Prettier, too. Her eyelashes were long and dark on her cheeks and . . .

He bent forward as though about to kiss her. Suddenly he turned around and flopped on the long leather transom beside the desk. Presently he slept.

CHAPTER FIVE

ONE MEANS OF ESCAPE

A T ten o'clock the next morning, Jimmy Vance was a very busy young man. His sleeves were rolled up, his tie was awry, his hat was shoved far back on his head and his nose bore a smudge of grease.

The *Shanung* lay in the quiet blue sea, decks aslant, entirely too peaceful for a ship which had so recently been the scene of terrible carnage.

From the boat deck, Jimmy could see far and he stopped often to study the horizon. He was expecting either a plane or small boats. Now that Burt knew where they were, Pete Gar would not be long in coming.

The engine of a small launch was the target of Jimmy's restless energy. For some reason best known to the men who had pirated this boat, the launch still lay in her davits. But the one-cylinder engine was rusted, the tank was empty of gas, and the carburetor lay in several discarded pieces about the mount.

Virginia Rockham, her Cossack jacket only a little rumpled, sat on the gunwale, watching Jimmy. She, too, kept a lookout.

"Is there any hope for it?" said Virginia.

"The patient ought to come out of the ether some time this afternoon," replied Jimmy. "I've done everything in the world but fix motorboat engines. That's been a blank spot in my education."

"Say, couldn't we row?"

"Sure, only what would we do for oars?"

"I didn't think of that," said Virginia, inspiration dying out of her eyes.

Jimmy picked up a hammer and straightened out a bolt, wishing he could take the hammer to the whole affair. No wonder they'd left this launch behind!

"What will they do if they catch us here?" asked Virginia.

"If I listed all the things they might do to us, I'd never get this engine finished and you'd faint. Stop worrying about it. They either will or won't. And the least they will do is kill us. I know too much. You know too much. Burt didn't have the guts, but Pete Gar will be along and he's not shy on anything but brains."

"Oh," said Virginia, sweeping the horizon again, her dark eyes worried.

After a bit she fell to studying Jimmy's back. Jimmy was not necessarily what is known as a strong man. He was neither tall nor silent nor handsomely bronzed. His face was narrow and combative and he had a very belligerent nose. His eyes were the mirrors and barometers of his emotions and they changed as swiftly as a glass before a typhoon.

Virginia decided that she had never known anyone quite like Jimmy. She had known a few who possessed the component parts: energy, vitality, a tongue which rolled out words as if they were a barrage of heavy artillery.

Unexpectedly, she asked, "Jimmy, how much do you make on the *Oriental Press?*"

He looked up, stopped work and gave her a very amused smile. "Not enough to buy your face powder."

"Oh . . . Oh, I didn't mean that!" She blushed in confusion.

"I make forty dollars a week and some of my expenses. I buy a new suit every six months. I don't like spinach. I live by myself and have a number one boy who loafs and smokes opium. I was born many years ago in a town you've never heard of, in a state where they grow wheat and then more wheat and complain about the government. I drink, gamble and smoke cigarettes." Abruptly he went back to work.

"You're mean," accused Virginia. "All I was thinking about was what you were doing now. Out here, ready to be gobbled up by people you don't even know, working on a story which couldn't have so very much interest to you. Or profit either, since you turn down my offer."

"I'm out here for the story," replied Jimmy. "I make my own assignments and write them myself. I'd trade my shirt for a byline any day because my name looks pretty in print. As for the reward, well, we may find Rockham, but I haven't any faith in the time limit."

"Oh," said Virginia.

"No," replied Jimmy. "Any idea what you're going to do if the Rockham billions shoot the chutes?"

"Why, no, I . . . I guess I'd find myself a job."

"As what?" said Jimmy.

"As a . . . a stenographer, I suppose."

"Do you know typing or shorthand?"

"No, but . . ."

"Then I guess we'd better find old man Rockham before the works go out from under him. But, to be less brutal, that isn't why I'm so darned keen on finding Rockham. Not because I can't live without getting the story—though a story's usually everything, you know—but because China would be in a bad way if his interests were split up. There's his foundation up north. That would fold if his fortune went and flood relief would collapse. Factions fighting for Rockham's property would split China into twenty pieces. If we fail to find your father, former civil wars won't be anything to what we'll face. I've thrown my lot with China. I know China and I'm respected by China. Back home they remember me as a kid in knickers—that bad little Vance boy. Rockham's death would pull out the bottom from the silver market, the oil market, and, by God, I'm not going to see my friends—and I don't care if they are yellow skinned—pitched all ways from the center just because one man held too much power."

A little grimly, he went back to work. Virginia said nothing. She was seeing her father in an entirely different light. Rockham had been just a father to her. True he had always been generous with money, had treated her indulgently. But she had never quite realized the power he had held.

Then she knew that it was not just a matter of markets, but of human beings. Suddenly her eagerness to find Rockham doubled—and she had thought that that was impossible.

Jimmy worked late into the afternoon and then, weary and grease-stained, he retired to the captain's cabin and opened a few cans in the adjoining pantry. Virginia stood by, helplessly, trying to aid him. She cut her finger on a ragged edge of tin and stepped back, wisely quitting a job she did not know.

However, after they had finished their supper, she did wash the dishes, breaking only one. She was finding out something new.

"On forty dollars a week," said Jimmy, "a newshawk's wife has to learn a lot." He grinned maliciously and settled himself in the captain's armchair.

The twilight was fading into blackness. The sounds of the ship were growing more and more pronounced. The groaning hulk whispered of the dead.

CHAPTER SIX

YELLOW PIRATES

L ATE the following morning, Jimmy completed the task of practically rebuilding the engine. While the launch still lay in the davits, he pulled the flywheel around time after time in an earnest hope that the rebuilding was not in vain.

Virginia stood by, murmuring consolation from time to time, feeling like a one-woman cheering gallery.

Exasperated at the repeated failure, Jimmy stood up and stretched his aching back. His right hand was blistered and the blisters had broken.

"Go on aft," ordered Jimmy, "and see what you can see."

Meekly she went to do his bidding. The stern of the ship was pointing toward that low-lying fringe on the rim of the sea which would be land. She heard the grind and chug of Jimmy's efforts and leaned against the top deck rail, watching the sea.

Suddenly a speck made itself apparent against the fringe. The sun made a haze of light over the water and it was not easy to see through the glaring sparkle, but she was certain that the speck was there. For minutes she watched it and then decided that the thing was moving. At least it was growing in size.

She hastened forward to the bridge, passing Jimmy, and

procured a pair of field glasses. With these she returned to the deck.

"Spot anything?" said Jimmy from the launch.

"Maybe," replied Virginia. "I was going to make certain before I called you."

He dropped down to the deck, took the glasses from her and strode aft. He focused the long barrels and directed them toward the speck.

Suddenly he gasped and his eyes flamed. "My God! That's a seagoing junk and it's heading straight for us!"

"You . . . you mean it's pirates?"

"No telling what I mean. It's my guess Pete Gar has arrived."

"But . . . but the launch won't start!"

Jimmy compressed his lips and scowled at the boat. "It'll start all right."

With this new incentive to drive him on, Jimmy found a long belt. His hands were too raw to permit further cranking with the handle. He wrapped the belt around the flywheel in such a way that when he pulled it, the wheel would spin many times.

Minutes fled. The speck grew into a hull and mast and sails. Brass glittered along the rails of the approaching junk. The slowness with which it came gave Jimmy the encouragement he needed.

He changed the carburetor, primed the cylinder and gave one big yank. The engine went into boisterous life. The launch shook. The propeller whirled without anything to cut down its speed.

In spite of the vibration and the need for haste, Jimmy let the engine warm. He cut loose the lashing and swung the davits out. He prepared to lower away.

"Before we go," said Jimmy, "I'm going to take one final look about this ship. I've been working so hard on this engine I haven't had time and I may need some dope for the story I intend to write. Local color." He smiled at her and vanished, leaving her to watch the inexorable approach of the junk.

In the bow she could make out twin brass cannon of ancient type. She could see the colored jackets of men on the decks. She could even see the ripple of white water under the oncoming bows.

Down below, Jimmy went to the cabin which had been occupied by Rockham. The trunks were broken open and their contents were strewn across the room. Dress shirts were tangled with tweeds, hats were bashed in and thrown down, a pair of military brushes had been cast aside.

Jimmy had looked in here on the first day aboard and he had seen some things which might be of later use. He had seen very puzzling things.

For instance, the pearl studs had been left where they lay in spite of their value. A small bag in the corner had disclosed a sheaf of bills, several diamond stickpins and numerous letters. Jimmy took them all. He pinned the jewelry on the inside of his undershirt, out of sight. He placed the bills in his money belt, and he thrust the letters into his pocket.

That done he went back on deck and began the task of lowering the launch into the water. Virginia held one tackle line, Jimmy managed the other. The boat dropped evenly into the blue sea.

The junk had come much closer, but that had been Jimmy's intention. It would be impossible to outsail the Chinese ship if it had time to change its course and intercept them.

A yell floated across the water to them. The Chinese could see what was taking place. Jimmy wrapped the belt about the flywheel and started the engine again.

Virginia waited for the start with held breath. Everything depended upon a small mechanism she had so recently seen in scattered pieces.

The engine roared alive. Jimmy stood up in the stern, holding the tiller. The launch swerved away from the *Shanung*, went around in a frothy curve and headed for the beach.

Another yell sounded aboard the junk. Men ran aft to the sculling oars and the Chinese counterpart of the galleon changed its course back to the beach.

The big brown sail flapped in the wind. The square bows with their great staring eyes of paint and wood headed out in the path of the launch.

Less than five hundred yards separated the two boats and Jimmy looked back with a certain cold calculation in his eyes, which made Virginia wonder how he could be so calm.

The brown sail filled out in the crosswind. Men at the sculling oars shouted to keep in time and the mammoth twin sweeps went back and forth, back and forth, leaving whirlpools tinged with white froth on the face of the sea.

"They're pirates all right," said Jimmy. "Funny, I thought . . ." He stopped and looked to the engine.

The launch was making a bare six knots and the junk was doing all of that. Virginia sat very still, facing Jimmy, looking past him at the following boat. The thing looked like a great brown vulture on the blue seas. Only that hammering engine would keep them out of the vulture's claws.

Jimmy watched their course. The field glasses dangled about his neck, tossing back and forth as the swells rocked them.

"Never did like pirates," said Jimmy. "I was stopped by them once up north of Canton. I bought them out."

Virginia looked up at his face. "Bought them out?"

"Yeah, in a way. I bet the leader I was a better pistol shot than he was and he fell for it. I was much better. We buried him."

"But," said Virginia, "you won't be able to do anything like that this time, will you?"

"Who knows? Who knows? The hand is quicker than the eye and the ring of gold is louder than steel, and a rolling stone picks up lots of tricks. I don't know who this is except that he's a pirate on Bias Bay, which should be a quick sufficient index of his colossal wickedness.

"There always have been pirates on Bias Bay and there always will be. And they're worse when they use modern weapons."

"But don't they patrol the area?" asked Virginia.

"Sure they do, but this is a pretty big place."

"Then we might locate a gunboat!"

"Excellent, excellent. Progress to Grade B. I'm now busily engaged in searching for said gunboat."

Virginia felt better until it became apparent that they were

43

not holding their own against the brown vulture. Then her heart began to pound heavily and her throat contracted.

"They're gaining," she said.

Jimmy turned around and looked at the junk. "I guess they are."

The irregular splutter of the launch engine was growing monotonous. But Virginia caught herself listening for a stray sound which might foretell a breakdown. She couldn't tell, of course, but she listened just the same. She had had plenty of experience with motors in her life. She was far more at home in a car than in a kitchen.

Excitement flashed across Jimmy's face. He pointed ahead and then picked up the glasses and studied the shoreline.

"Yep, it's a gunboat!"

Joy surged through Virginia like a drink of wine. "Where?"

"Right under that headland. She's lying at anchor and I can't seem to locate her flag, but she's a gunboat just the same."

Jimmy turned and looked back at the Chinese junk. He felt uneasy for a moment. Obviously the junk could also sight the gunboat. Why then did it persist in driving on in toward it?

The launch engine was throwing off fumes from its hot cylinder. A clanking sound was apparent in the otherwise steady roar.

Jimmy frowned at the rusty machinery as much as to promise it a good beating should it fail on them.

They swept in upon the beach, heading straight for the gunboat which was still a mile distant from them. Virginia had the feeling that they would never make it. Virginia was right.

The engine stopped with a wheezing sigh, kicked over once and stopped again.

The junk swept down upon them, growing larger by the second. Jimmy dropped beside the engine and tried to fix the belt over the flywheel again.

Abruptly the junk towered over them, its weathered planking rising like a tower above the smaller boat. The sculling oars were sweeping back and forth in a mad attempt to reverse and stop the headway.

A man with a lean, somehow feline face stared down at them. He held an ancient horse pistol in his hand, lifted up as though a throwing motion was necessary to discharge the ball. He had a thin mustache and his eyes were queerly green. His teeth were ragged, yellower than his sunken cheeks.

He was dressed in a red jacket which flapped about his washboard ribs and wore a straw coolie hat on the back of his head. But for all the cheapness of his garb, he looked powerful.

"Ai!" he cried, and then in rapid Shantung Chinese, "Throw us your rope or I blow you into the Seventh Hell!"

Jimmy, with a wry look at Virginia, complied. The rope was instantly made fast by a puffy-faced sailor who was dressed in nothing more than a ragged pair of pants.

"Now come up!" cried the pirate.

Jimmy, with all the viciousness of the Shantung language at his command, managed to swallow the words which threatened to pour out.

*A man with a lean, somehow feline face stared down
at them. He held an ancient horse pistol in his hand,
lifted up as though a throwing motion was
necessary to discharge the ball.*

He helped Virginia up to the deck and then followed her. When he reached the planking of the malodorous ship, he looked the pirate squarely in the eye, studying him. Then, as though he had seen something which left a bad taste in his mouth, he deliberately spat over the rail.

The Chinese insult was almost too much for the pirate. He screamed for his men to take these Foreign Devils aft to the great cabin.

Jimmy needed no taking. He guided Virginia through the gaping men and across coiled ropes and stores and let her pass through the cabin door before him.

Then Jimmy sighed. "Well, we didn't make it, did we?"

CHAPTER SEVEN

WHERE IS ROCKHAM?

THE after cabins of the junk were entirely out of keeping with the mangy appearance of the vessel. Here were great silk panels, blackwood furnishings, gold incense burners from which came the tang of sandalwood, cushions, and fine North China rugs.

Virginia looked about her, bewildered. This was a far cry from the Western world and she had been in the Orient for months, but not until now had she fully realized her presence there. This was the East as she had thought of it.

The pirate entered behind them, still carrying the horse pistol in his uplifted hand. He looked long at Jimmy and then turned his beady-eyed attention to the girl. All his movements had the effortless quality of a cat's.

"I," said the pirate, "am Lee Chang." He waited for some change in their expressions which would signify that they had heard the name. But as Virginia did not understand Shantung Chinese and as Jimmy wore a masklike expression, no change was apparent.

"Ah," said Lee Chang, "you have not heard of me. Then perhaps I can refresh your minds. I am the king of the Bias Bay pirates, the monarch over death. I travel hand in hand with all the devils of the Black World. Well? What have you to say to that?"

"Nothing," replied Jimmy.

"What were you doing aboard the . . . the *Shanung*?" demanded Lee Chang. "To what faction do you belong? Who are you?"

"I am from the *Oriental Press*," replied Jimmy.

"Ah," said Lee Chang, a greenish light coming into his eyes. "You are down here to spy upon us, to bring the gunboats down upon us. You are here and now that you are, I fear that the *Oriental Press* will lose a perhaps valued man. As for your woman . . ." He smiled a feline smile at Virginia and she edged closer to Jimmy.

"I know a great deal," said Lee Chang. "My spies are everywhere. My band extends to Shanghai and to Hong Kong. I am a power and my word is law to thousands. Well? You do not seem to be impressed. Perhaps I can best demonstrate my power by killing you . . . very . . . very slowly."

"All this talk," said Jimmy, "is wasted. You do not intend to kill us immediately. You are seeking something. What is it?"

Lee Chang smiled, "The Foreign Devil is acute. Very acute. Yes, I want to know something which you can doubtless tell me. Twice I have made the trip to the ruined *Shanung*."

"Once to gut her and twice to . . . ?"

Lee Chang stiffened in anger. "I did not pirate the *Shanung*!"

Jimmy blinked. "Then what are you trying to do now? If you had nothing to do with that robbery, why are you interested in it?"

"You want to know too much," snapped Lee Chang.

"Yes, I do at that," said Jimmy.

"And you know too much. Were you aboard the *Shanung* when that vessel was attacked?"

It seemed to Jimmy that the pirate leaned forward expectantly, waiting for the answer. Sparring for time, Jimmy remained silent.

"Were you aboard her? Were you?"

"No," said Jimmy.

"Were you part of the attacking party?" Lee Chang waved the pistol belligerently. "Were you?"

"No," said Jimmy.

"Ah, you expect me to believe lies. Lies! Do you know who I am? Do you know that I could kill you as you stand there? Do not trifle with the truth."

"I had nothing to do with it," said Jimmy.

"Bah!"

"Yeah, bah! Listen, you fool. I am Jimmy Vance of the *Oriental Press,* see? I am the man who writes the news. I am on the trail of news. I haven't anything to do with any petty squabble of yours. To me you're just a pirate and a lousy pirate at that. If you haven't any better sense than to stand there posing in front of me, go back and find out what you want to know on the *Shanung.* Don't ask me unless you want to believe me."

Lee Chang quivered and worked his jaw. He looked at Virginia and then realized by the blank expression in her eyes that she understood none of this.

"Bah!" cried Lee Chang. "If you weren't there, then why were you there when I went out?"

"Because, like you," said Jimmy, taking a potshot at random, "I want to know who did this thing. Perhaps you have heard of a newspaper someplace?"

Lee Chang thrust the horse pistol in his belt and shrugged his scarlet jacket solidly into place about his thin shoulders. "You place me in a very bad position. I want information, so do you. You undoubtedly know a great deal. Therefore, it is imperative that I examine your mind."

Jimmy knew that he meant torture, but the knowledge did not show upon his face. "Who or what are you looking for?"

Lee Chang glared. "The American billionaire, of course! Ah, I could get a million dollars in ransom for him. I could go to Kowloon and start my own gambling houses on the money. And yet, I cannot so much as find one single trace of the man!"

Jimmy wanted to laugh, but he kept a very sober mien. "You mean the oil merchant, the American. I am also looking for him. He is not to be found, though his baggage is still aboard the *Shanung*. The others must have him."

"Bah, these others! I know nothing of them."

"You certainly should know something," replied Jimmy. "They have invaded your territory. They have committed a crime for which you might very well hang. Do you think the courts would believe that you did not pirate the *Shanung*? You would die for this crime."

Lee Chang frowned. It was apparent that he had not thought of that before.

Jimmy plunged on. "This Rockham is a famous man. He

STORIES from the GOLDEN AGE

☐ Yes, I would like to receive my **FREE CATALOG** featuring all 80 volumes of the *Stories from the Golden Age Collection* and more!

Name _____

Shipping Address _____

City _____ State _____ ZIP _____

Telephone _____ E-mail _____

Check other genres you are interested in: ☐ SciFi/Fantasy ☐ Western ☐ Mystery

FREE SHIPPING!
NO PURCHASE REQUIRED

6 Books • 8 Stories
Illustrations • Glossaries

6 Audiobooks • 12 CDs
8 Stories • Full color 40-page booklet

Fold on line and tape

IF YOU ENJOYED READING THIS BOOK, GET THE ACTION/ADVENTURE COLLECTION AND SAVE 25%

BOOK SET	**AUDIOBOOK SET**
~~$59.50~~ $45.00	~~$77.50~~ $58.00
ISBN: 978-1-61986-089-6	ISBN: 978-1-61986-090-2

☐ Check here if shipping address is same as billing.

Name _____

Billing Address _____

City _____ State _____ ZIP _____

Telephone _____ E-mail _____

Credit/Debit Card #: _____

Card ID # (last 3 or 4 digits): _____

Exp Date: ____/____ Date (month/day/year): ____/____/____

Order Total *(CA and FL residents add sales tax)*: _____

To order online, go to: **www.GoldenAgeStories.com** or call toll-free **1-877-8GALAXY** or 1-323-466-7815

owns nations body and soul. Do you think the nations will fail to send gunboats as soon as they are certain Rockham disappeared in Bias Bay? Gunboats are already on the way down here. I have already sent out the word that I have found the *Shanung*. You are the most famous of all pirates, therefore is it not logical that they would spare no effort at catching you and putting you to death? And all for a crime others have done. You must take all the danger and you receive none of the profits."

Lee Chang's eyes were growing large. Quite obviously all this was a new thought. "You," he said, "are a very clever man. You know the outside world. I do not. If I were to keep you here, you could tell me much." He paused and then his voice became sharp. "But how do I know that you are not lying? There is only one way to find that out. I have certain mechanisms for the purpose of extracting truth. Perhaps . . ."

Lee Chang turned and went out, head bowed in thought. Jimmy heard the lock turn, heard mumbled orders which posted the guard outside.

"He sounded angry," said Virginia. "What's happened?"

"I tried to wake up his professional pride," said Jimmy. "I don't know how well I succeeded. A few hours will tell. He'll either come back here and take us apart or he'll be willing to listen to me."

"Has he got Dad?"

"No," said Jimmy. "That's the funny part of it. He hasn't and he doesn't seem to know where Rockham is. Rockham means money to him and he's sore about it. Time will tell,

Virginia, time will tell. It's tough on you to have to run into all this."

"Oh, never mind about me, Jimmy. I can take it. But I'm worried sick over what might have happened to Dad. *Where is he?*"

CHAPTER EIGHT

"Don't Be Afraid
to Kill Her!"

DUSK came before the sculling oars ceased their endless complaints. Ropes whispered forward and bare feet padded over the deck of the junk.

Jimmy went to the mammoth stern ports and pushed aside a drapery which hung there. He saw the fiery sky and the dark sea blending on the horizon and then his interest quickened.

Hull down to the south lay the gunboat. Jimmy, regarding the vessel, fumed. "What do they think the government's paying them for, anyway? To look pretty? Damn their hides, they haven't even looked over this way to investigate this junk."

"Maybe they think this is just a fishing boat," said Virginia.

"With all these brass cannon showing? Say, this thing's as obviously pirate as galleons were Spanish."

"Couldn't we get word to them somehow?"

"How? The instant they miss us, they'd start in pursuit. What would we use to get there? Wings?"

Virginia pointed down at the water under the ports. Three sampans and their confiscated launch were dragging in the ripples behind the junk. The oars were shipped in the unique grass huts which covered the 'midships sections.

"They'd know we were gone," protested Jimmy, "and they'd know where we went and after that they'd have no trouble at all catching up with us. That's out."

"But if one of us stayed here . . ."

Jimmy scowled a moment and then looked at the canopied bunk which was partially covered by curtains. Then he shook his head. "I couldn't leave you here."

"I'm not afraid," said Virginia.

Jimmy walked restless across the rug and then turned on her, his eyes alight with sudden enthusiasm. "Listen here. Can you row?"

"Why, certainly I can row."

"Then, that's it! You slide down that rope and take the first sampan right after dark. You'll have to scull because I don't see any oarlocks. But the distance isn't so far and if they thought you were still here, you could make it. Then you could tell that gunboat where I am and they could come across and earn some of their pay. Is it a bargain?"

"I . . . I hate to leave you."

"Somebody will have to cover your retreat. And you'll have to bring them back fast in case the deception doesn't work out the way it's supposed to. Quick, Virginia, I'll lower you. It's too dark for them to see right now!"

Her hand clutched and held his sleeve. Her eyes were dark, somehow wistful. "I . . ."

Jimmy caught her shoulders, gave her a little shake, and then reached out of the port and dragged the sampan close under the overhanging stern.

Now that matters had fairly begun, Virginia's hand shook. But she was game. She let Jimmy lower her out of the ports. She kicked about until the thwarts of the sampan were under her feet and then dropped silently down.

She picked up an oar and thrust it through the stern thole. It was almost dark with the swift tropical night coming down upon the water like so much black dust. She unfastened the painter and took her post in the stern.

The sampan drifted clear. By the light of a great lantern she could see the shaven heads of two pirates who sat on the afterdeck eating rice out of small bowls, using chopsticks to stuff their overcrowded mouths.

In her excitement she forgot that the lantern light could not reach this far. But she knew that she dared not start sculling now. Any slight sound would prove disastrous.

She heard a voice over her head. It was that of Lee Chang and it sounded like the crackle of small fireworks. She heard Jimmy's swift reply and then a shout.

She waited to hear no more. Digging the oar into the water she moved it quickly back and forth, facing forward and watching for the twinkle of lights which would mark the gunboat.

No more sounds came from the junk. She did not know if Jimmy had run into trouble through their move. She did not know what had taken place. Fear for Jimmy lent strength to her arms.

She had done this sculling many times before in her life. It was an old trick, used when an oar was missing. The sampan lurched under the steady drive of the blade, sweeping forward to the tune of the gurgling water under the hull.

From the grass hut forward came the odor of decomposed fish. She wished the wind would blow the other way.

The junk was far behind her, marked only by a flicker of the yellow lantern. Occasionally she stared back, anxiety creating a lump in her throat.

Each time she was tempted to stop and rest, she thought of Jimmy, and drove the oar the harder. Her hands, unused to such work, felt like they had been burned. Her small back ached with the repeated swing. Her eyes hurt from staring ahead at the cluster of sparks which marked the presence of the gunboat.

If anything happened to Jimmy it would be all her fault.

She had brought him into this. Rockham was her father, not Jimmy's. And yet Jimmy had stayed behind to cover her retreat and had smiled when he did it, quite as though it had been nothing more grave than helping her with her coat.

A growing suspicion came over her. Maybe Jimmy knew what they were up against. But no, she had seen this boat for him. She had suggested the idea. Why had she thought of it? The further she went through the lonely darkness, the less she liked the plan. It would have been far more honorable to have stayed there instead of running away and letting Jimmy take the consequences for her.

He was such a swell guy, that Jimmy. Admiration took the place of some of her fears. Faith in Jimmy supplanted some of her doubts. Maybe he could talk Lee Chang out of any violence.

And then a thought hit her that made her stop sculling. If they had discovered the absence of the sampan and her escape, they would know where she was going. And knowing that they could not hope to stand up against a gunboat, they would hide themselves in one of any number of small bays along the shore. They would take him inland. Perhaps she would never see him again!

The thought was suffocating. "Oh, Jimmy, Jimmy, why did I go?"

She sent the sampan ahead at a swifter pace. She'd have to get the gunboat on the scene before any thought like that occurred to Lee Chang.

The twinkling lights were brighter now. They sent long golden streamers out to meet her. The lights were friendly, calling to her.

At last the dark hull loomed over her. The sampan, moving sluggishly now, bobbed in through the swell toward the landing stage.

Virginia was exhausted. It had been such a long way. She knew she never could have made it if Jimmy had not been the stake.

A tall, yellow-skinned Chinese leaned off the stage and grabbed the sampan's painter. He made it fast and then with a boathook he drew the stern into the glare of a landing light. His only comment upon seeing Virginia was a grunt.

"Must be a Chinese Navy boat," thought Virginia. "I . . . I hope they can speak English."

Panting, she made her way past the man on watch and up the ladder to the deck. Everything was quiet there. Several sailors lounged against a bulkhead. They eyed her almost without interest. It was not until then that she noticed their lack of uniforms. But then the Chinese Navy had never been renowned for neatness and order. All Virginia wanted was a few workable guns.

The bridge glittered with light. She went to the ladder and started up. No officers were in sight. Something of the coolness began to affect her. What was wrong here?

She had expected to stagger aboard and blurt out her story immediately, but now that no one was here, what would she do?

She saw a closed door under which a slit of light was visible. This was probably the captain's room. Timidly she knocked.

A very polite voice called out something in Chinese which she took to be a command to enter. She opened the door and stepped through, momentarily blinded by the harsh light in the cabin.

A man in a black robe stood up out of his chair. Amazement flashed across his face. Then he bowed and smiled a small smile which did not make her at all welcome.

"May I ask who you are?" said this gentleman of undetermined race.

"I am Virginia Rockham," she replied. "I have come to demand your services."

"Services?" he said, a mocking note in his otherwise smooth voice. "But before we go into that, do you not wish to know who I might happen to be?"

"Why . . . why, yes," said Virginia, suddenly assailed by doubts.

"In Shanghai, I am known as Cheng. Nothing more. Merely Cheng. It is hardly a suitable index to me but it will suffice, eh?"

Virginia knew nothing about Cheng. Jimmy could have told her that Cheng was supposed to be some kind of unofficial ambassador from Manchukuo, but there would have been doubt in Jimmy's voice.

"You mean . . . You are captain here, are you not? And judging from the armament here, this is a gunboat, is it not?" Virginia covered her fear with a dignified bearing.

"Ah, you are right on both counts, Miss Rockham. That is correct, is it? Miss Rockham."

"Certainly."

"The daughter of the great George Harley Rockham?"

"Certainly!"

"Ah," said Cheng, rubbing his small yellow hands. Then he very carefully reached across the desk and picked up a brass hammer. With this he struck a vibrant note on a small bell.

Unable to understand all this, Virginia stared at him. The man was somehow unclean. Her fears trebled and she hid her hands behind her because she could feel them shake.

Presently the cabin door opened. A scarred white face peered in. The ugly mouth wreathed into a smile. Virginia backed hastily away.

"Pete Gar!" she whispered.

Pete Gar smiled and stepped toward her, hands outstretched.

"Pete," said Cheng. "Hold this lady's arms while I talk with her. Perhaps she will need a little coercion to answer some of my questions."

Virginia whirled on Cheng. Pete caught her arms deftly behind her and gave them a quick wrench just to show her that the grip could hurt.

A spasm of pain went across her face. She turned very white.

"Miss Rockham," snapped Cheng, no longer smooth, *"where is your father?"*

Virginia stiffened and Pete twisted her arms again. "I don't know! I don't know!"

Cheng's long-nailed finger shook before her face. "Answer me quickly. Where is George Harley Rockham? Don't be afraid to hurt her, you fool, break her arms if necessary. I've got to know!"

Pete grinned and applied the pressure once more.

CHAPTER NINE

Jimmy Faces Torture

AFTER Virginia had disappeared through the stern ports, Jimmy carefully closed the glass in spite of the heat. He had already heard the footsteps outside his door.

With a quick jerk of his wrist he threw the curtains across the front of the bunk and when the door opened, the Chinese found him peacefully seated in a blackwood chair gazing innocently at the ceiling.

"I thought I heard a sound," said Lee Chang, his feline face quivering suspiciously.

"The evil have bad dreams," replied Jimmy, still looking at the ceiling. "But lower your voice, Lee Chang. The lady is tired. She sleeps." He indicated the bunk.

"Quiet? You ask me to be quiet on my own ship?" roared Lee Chang. "You are an insolent wretch!" He went back to the entrance, somewhat undecided. "But never mind. I send men ashore to find out what they can. If I discover that you know anything about this wealthy Foreign Devil I shall take great delight in slitting your throat and watching the blood run."

Jimmy's blood was already running—cold. If they discovered the absence of the sampan they would know that the girl was gone. He must prevent that. They could overtake her in a very short while.

63

For once in his life, words stuck in his glib throat. "Er...uh. Why is this Foreign Devil so important to you?"

"Money, you fool! Money. I need it badly. Do you think I wish to live forever on this sea?"

Lee Chang was gone before Jimmy could say anything else. Feet padded on the worn decks. Men moved back and forth, shifting gear, evidently making ready to put to sea on a moment's notice should the occasion arise.

Jimmy almost forgot to breathe. Any minute now he'd hear their yell and the junk would up anchor and streak after the sampan. It would be easy to find it, too. It would lie somewhere along a straight line drawn between the pirate boat and the gunboat.

As minutes passed he began to feel better. No yells yet. And when a half-hour had lagged by, he was almost normal. He stood up and mopped his brow. Even if they took after the girl now, they wouldn't overtake her.

And then the yell came. It was high-pitched, directly over Jimmy's head. Feet slapped excitedly upon the planks. Suddenly the cabin door was flung back and Lee Chang marched in, bristling, quivering with intense anger.

By the light of the swinging peanut-oil lamp which hung from the beams, Lee Chang's face looked cruel and yellow and very angry.

"Where is that sampan?" cried Lee Chang.

"How should I know that?" countered Jimmy, standing up, his back to the bunk.

Lee Chang flung him to one side and darted forward.

His yellow claws raked aside the curtains, disclosing the unrumpled bed. "You lied to me! She is gone!"

"Yes, gone," snapped Jimmy. "You've been fooled, tricked like the dull-witted coolie you are. Now what the hell are you going to do about it?"

Lee Chang clutched at his red jacket. A dagger with a white jade handle came away from his washboard ribs. He drew back his lips.

Jimmy sprang to one side just as Lee Chang lunged. Jimmy's fist slapped solidly into the yellow jaw. Lee Chang rocketed against the table, upsetting its contents across the rug.

Three shaven-headed Chinese ran forward. Jimmy turned on them. He gripped the hanging lamp and swung himself back. Before the first man could dodge, Jimmy's heels smashed his chest.

Lee Chang leaped up, spitting curses and blood and fragments of teeth. The dagger was gleaming again. The remaining two sailors closed swiftly in upon Jimmy. One snatched at his legs, the other took his arms. Jimmy twisted violently, trying to throw them off. Lee Chang loomed above Jimmy. The knife blade was sharp against Jimmy's chest.

Recognizing defeat, Jimmy stopped his wriggling. Through his mind flashed the picture of Virginia setting out through darkness to reach the cruiser. Soon the cruiser would be upon the junk and all this would be over.

Another thought flashed across Jimmy's mind in that second. The four-day limit was up. Unless something happened, Rockham's interests would be swept up by the time the market opened in Wall Street in the morning. Virginia would be left a pauper in the Asiatic—a fate which had only one answer.

Damn a man's power when it was no more united or organized than that. Rockham's speculations and interests were based on clay. His Chinese oil monopoly would be no more.

Lee Chang's voice was twisted with rage. "Why have you done this? Do not answer me. I know why. You are trying to keep me from reaching Rockham. Where is he? You know that. Where is he?"

"I don't know where he is," snapped Jimmy. "If you've got any sense, you know that the lady will reach that gunboat and that sailors and guns will be down upon you in a matter of hours."

"I can deal with their guns. And I can deal with the sailors." Lee Chang rocked back on his calloused heels, certain that Jimmy was held powerless by the two men. "It is a joke upon the lady and a joke upon you."

"What do you mean by that?"

"What I say. That vessel is not a gunboat. I know by way of my spies who came to me as soon as I anchored that the vessel committed the robbery of the *Shanung*. The prisoners of the *Shanung* are being held ashore."

"Then Rockham is . . . ?"

"This wealthy devil is not among them. No one knows just how he looks, but it is certain that he is not. Otherwise he would be pleading and offering his gold and no one is doing that." Lee Chang forgot his sore jaw and mouth. He laughed shrilly. "When the lady arrives on the vessel she thinks is a gunboat, they will place an immediate end to her."

66

"Good God!" cried Jimmy.

"It is a priceless joke," cackled Lee Chang. "A priceless joke." Then he leaned forward again. "But you tried to escape from me. You tried to have my vessel sunk by your prying sailors. For that . . ."

Lee Chang got to his feet and jerked his thumb toward the door. "Take him out on the deck. Perhaps we will have a little sport out of this after all. It is impossible to find this wealthy American. Everything is ruined, but I have become used to that."

Jimmy dug in his heels, attempting to halt their progress to the deck. But the sailors were stronger than he had thought. They shoved him easily ahead.

Lee Chang marched in advance. The remainder of the crew clustered about the circle of light left by the great lantern. Their heads were shaven and their faces were hungry and watchful. They were a ragged lot.

Lee Chang looked at them and then said in surprisingly perfect English, "One would never believe that an educated man would have such a crew at his command."

Jimmy started violently. Lee Chang's eyes had a flicker of insanity in them. He was one of those rare specimens, Jimmy guessed, who had a perfect right to live in the best of society, but who worked out a grudge against the world through crime.

"You are surprised, eh?" said Lee Chang, still in English. "I do not doubt that. I was educated by a missionary and I killed him and took his money when the courses were finished. You wonder now why I am powerful in Bias Bay, why my name is so great here? It is because I am educated—in many, many things, such as . . ." He smiled and let the sentence hang. His scarlet jacket flapped in the night wind against his lean ribs.

Lee Chang pointed up at the gaff, outlined against the stars. A sailor hastily brought a rope from it and gave it to the pirate captain. Lee Chang jerked Jimmy's hand out and held it in very strong fingers. The rope went about the thumb. Lee Chang called for another rope and this was instantly made fast to Jimmy's left hand.

Without a word the sailors took in the slack. Jimmy's arms were lifted high over his head. He glared at the pirate.

"Now," said Lee Chang, relapsing into Chinese, "I shall cause you to be hoisted up until your feet clear the deck. Then I shall take this very sharp knife and begin to slit you a little at a time. Have you ever seen a carcass skinned? That is the way."

Jimmy watched the knife. Lee Chang gripped Jimmy's collar and the shirt was ripped wide down the back and front. Lee Chang touched Jimmy's chest with the knife point and drew down.

The pain was like a flash of white lightning. Jimmy gritted his teeth and strove to reach the deck with his toes. The pain in his hands was growing with every passing second.

It was all over now. He couldn't help Virginia. It was impossible to get out of this. No gunboat, nothing. And he hadn't even found Rockham. It hurt Jimmy to fail.

The knife went up again and came down in a quick slash. The dribble of blood was hot against Jimmy's bare flesh.

Suddenly, Lee Chang emitted a sharp cry. He leaned forward, staring at Jimmy's undershirt. He had seen a sparkle lying in the tattered fragments.

Instantly his long-nailed fingers ripped the cotton away. The blue fire of diamonds flashed in the pirate's face. The men strained forward, muttering at the beauty of the stickpins.

Lee Chang glanced up at Jimmy, his eyes bearing a puzzled expression. "What are these you have hidden from me?"

"What do they look like," spat Jimmy, white with pain. "Rock candy?"

"You have others like this?" hissed Lee Chang.

"Trunks full of them," snapped Jimmy.

"Ah," said Lee Chang. He padded aft into the stern cabins and came out presently, holding Jimmy's coat. By the light of the great lantern, Lee Chang fished through the pockets. The studs came to light and were admired. And then Lee Chang began to extract papers from the inner breast pocket.

Jimmy's heart began to beat once again. In spite of his pain, he could not help a swift grin, though the grin was prompted by bitter reflection.

Another thought flashed through Jimmy's mind. Where was Rockham? Jimmy couldn't believe the simplicity of it. Certainly these others would also stumble on the only obvious truth. If Rockham still lived, then Jimmy thought he could find him.

"What are these?" cried Lee Chang, dancing about in his excitement. "What are these?"

"Papers," said Jimmy with heavy sarcasm.

"Yes, papers! Letters. And they are all addressed to George Harley Rockham. Every one of them. I find no papers here but those addressed to him. What does this mean?"

"You guess, I've had my two turns."

Lee Chang swept the words aside with an impatient thrust of his hand. "You devil! You devil! You have been holding all this from me just because of your worthless gold. You have been more willing to lose your life than your money."

The knife flashed in two quick slashes and Jimmy dropped to the deck. "You," cried Lee Chang, "you are George Harley Rockham!"

Jimmy wanted to laugh in the pirate's face, but he managed to look betrayed. That George Harley Rockham would not be so young had not occurred to Lee Chang. But then it is always difficult to determine a foreigner's age. And obviously Lee Chang had never seen a picture of Rockham, much less Rockham in the flesh.

"And if I am?" said Jimmy.

"Then I get the ransom!" cried Lee Chang.

"But I'm not," said Jimmy, playing safe.

"Do not lie to me! Do not lie to me! I see everything now. What a fool I have been." Lee Chang danced about, first on one foot, then the other, waving his bright knife with its white jade handle. "You have billions! Billions! And I want millions only. You will get off light!"

Jimmy rubbed his thumbs. His chest was stinging terribly. But he still managed to look displeased.

And then a movement of lights came to him from far across the water.

The gunboat was getting underway! What would happen to Virginia now?

CHAPTER TEN

WOLVES TO THE KILL

JIMMY swore with great feeling. He moved along the low rail, staring at the gunboat. God only knew what would happen to Virginia now. The poor kid, worrying about him most likely, with plenty of worries of her own. It was certain that they would try to use her for a hostage if anything happened. It was also certain that they would think she knew more than she did.

He again saw Pete Gar's ugly face, Burt's stolidness, Joe's dumb features. Who, what, was behind all this anyway?

Lee Chang, still very excited, appointed a guard to watch the man "Rockham." Lee Chang was already laying plans as to how he would get the ransom. He was thinking about that gambling house he would run in Kowloon.

"Now what is wrong?" cried Lee Chang, seeing Jimmy's face.

Jimmy glared at him and then back at the gunboat.

"No," said Lee Chang, pretending to read his thoughts, "you can't save your filthy gold now."

Something clicked in Jimmy's brain. He swore more loudly and then sank down on a bitt, holding his head in his hands, a picture of despair.

"What is wrong?" demanded Lee Chang. "You have gold. Is that gold not worth your life?"

"Oh," said Jimmy. "Oh, oh, oh. The ransom I do not mind, but the *Shanung* . . ."

Lee Chang was instantly suspicious. "The *Shanung*?"

Jimmy nodded. "She still carries half a million dollars in gold bars and coin. I hid it aboard her. And now . . . now that other vessel is going out there . . . going out to get it!"

Lee Chang stared at the yellow lights. Jimmy watched the pirate's face, hardly daring to breathe. Would Lee Chang fall for it? Would he see through so thin a ruse? Would his gold madness blind him sufficiently?

Lee Chang's face showed no sign either way. His black eyes had a green light in them as he watched the gunboat. The soft whisper of the ground swells against the hull of the junk was the only sound in the night. Even the Chinese had stopped moving about, sensing something unusual in the air.

Jimmy writhed with the suspense of it. Would Lee Chang . . . ?

"Half a million in gold?" cried Lee Chang. "Half a million? Then . . . then that boat will get it! They'll steal it right under my nose. The dirty sons of pigs!"

Jimmy began to glow all over. It *had* worked.

Lee Chang whirled, scarlet jacket flapping. "Ho! Man the sweeps! Man the wheel! Man the sculls! We go back to the *Shanung*!"

Pirates scurried to do the bidding of their chief. In an amazingly short space of time, the anchor was up and the junk was heading out toward the anchored steamer. The sculls drove back and forth, leaving spinning whirlpools of phosphorescence. The sails groaned and flapped as they strove to scoop up the wind.

"It's folly," thought Jimmy. "But it's a try at least."

Presently Lee Chang strode restlessly by. Jimmy held up his hand. "You had best not attack those others. You have not sufficient men. You are not as fast as the gunboat. They will take the money and sink you."

"Yes?" cried Lee Chang. "Yes? That is what you think in your ignorance. They have no right in this bay. They have stolen a gunboat in the north and have come down here to take my right rewards. We shall see whether I am strong enough!" Quivering with anger, Lee Chang went away, still looking at the yellow patch of lights across the sea.

Jimmy smiled a little. This was only the start. He'd have to time things to the second. He'd have to make sure that everything was right before he went on.

When Lee Chang came by the second time, Jimmy said, "They will beat you to the *Shanung*. Your vessel is too slow. They will be there and will have gotten the gold and gone before you have reached the halfway mark."

"Yes?" cried Lee Chang, jumping about. "You think so! Man the third oar! Get some more sail on that mast!" He went down the deck, stamping and swearing.

Jimmy smiled once more. A puff of wind cooled his face and bare chest. He could not believe his own luck. If only he knew Virginia had not been hurt . . .

If Rockham was found tonight, then there would still be a chance to save the crumbling one-man empire. But if Lee

Chang discovered Jimmy's deception and came off with the day . . . Jimmy shuddered to think of it.

Once more he fell to pondering on the reasons behind all this. Something outside of Bias Bay was the moving force. In fact it had only been through a lucky break that they had found the *Shanung* at all. It might just as well have been in the Yellow Sea.

Gunboats of half a dozen nations were probably prowling the seas in search of the *Shanung* and Rockham. But the seas were large and the *Shanung* was small. No wonder the steamer had not been found. Jimmy gave thanks for Burt and Pete Gar. They had been useful in a way.

The junk forged onward, driven toward a dim shadow on the black water. The gunboat was far ahead of them, increasing its distance with every minute of sailing time.

When Lee Chang passed again, Jimmy said, "Since you are such a wolf, Lee Chang, don't you think you had better douse your lights? You might drive them off."

"Ah," said Lee Chang, and immediately barked a string of orders. The ship was instantly darkened. He turned back to Jimmy. "If you have lied about the gold bars . . ."

"I haven't lied," said Jimmy, innocently. "I am still worried about them."

In a few minutes, the lights of the gunboat were obscured. Jimmy knew that the vessel had passed on the other side of the *Shanung*. The junk was pitifully slow. Perhaps the gunboat would get away before they even touched the steamer.

Jimmy fell to wondering about what had happened to Virginia. A cold sweat stood out on his forehead as he remembered that the other prisoners of the *Shanung* were being held ashore. Perhaps Virginia was still ashore. He'd have to work that out when he came to it.

Jimmy's guard was ever near him, leaning on a short rifle, his eyes never long from Jimmy's back.

The *Shanung* suddenly materialized before them, outlined by the lights which flooded from the gunboat's deck. Spots of yellow roved the bridge. Forward in a bow port another light glowed, a flickering flame. Jimmy sighed with relief when he saw it.

Lee Chang was all stealth and viciousness. He eyed the two ships and spat into his scuppers.

"They're already unloading the gold," said Jimmy. "Do you see those lights up on the bridge?"

"The pigs!" rasped Lee Chang. "I shall give them no quarter. They have tried to take what is rightfully mine!"

The junk eased in beside the bow of the *Shanung*, close beside the gunboat. Lee Chang sent a whispered order down the deck, "Prepare to board!"

Men hunched ready under the rail, knives and rifles held in tight, sweaty hands. With a creak and bump, the junk came in beside the steamer. Iron hooks rattled, binding the two together.

"Boarders away!" shrieked Lee Chang. He gripped the rail over his head and went up to the steel deck.

A yellow howling avalanche shot out of the junk and deluged the *Shanung*. A rifle spat white fire in the night. Men cried out, voices thin against the roar. The lights on the *Shanung*'s bridge flashed down into the yelling horde.

Pirates stopped and emptied their guns in a swift volley. Then, holding their knives in their gleaming teeth, they swarmed up toward the bridge dodger.

A new sound entered the fray. From the gunboat came the howls of the gunboat crew. They scrambled over into the waist of the *Shanung,* their rags flapping, their knives ready. Suddenly the melee boiled into one vast fight. The pirates, fighting both front and rear, gave no quarter and expected none. Lee Chang discharged his horse pistol into the face of a gunboat sailor and then threw the smoking gun at another. Lee Chang's jade-handled dagger went swiftly to work like a flash of lightning.

Jimmy did not wait to see how things were coming out. As soon as the boarders were away, Jimmy whirled on his guard. The man threw up his rifle. It exploded straight down. Jimmy rapped the man's jaw with two sharp blows. The pirate staggered.

Without waiting to put a finishing blow through, Jimmy picked up the guard and flung him headlong into the sea. Jimmy snatched up the fallen rifle, strapped it across his back, and looked wildly at the gunboat.

He needed no second thought. His hand caught the bottom of the *Shanung's* rail. Hanging over the water he worked swiftly toward the gunboat. Above him the night was alight with exploding powder and torn asunder by yells of rage and agony.

The gunboat's deck was almost deserted when Jimmy reached it. A sailor stood at the helm, his yellow face twitching as he watched the fight. Another stood by the hawsers, ready to cast off.

Jimmy dropped down on the gunboat's deck. The man at the helm stared at him and then jerked up a revolver. Jimmy fired. A blue hole appeared in the Chinese shirt. The revolver came tumbling out of a bridge port. The sailor sagged over his wheel.

Jimmy caught the weapon before it hit the deck. It was better than a rifle for close work.

The man at the hawsers cried a warning which was lost in the thunder of the fight. He sprinted aft, a fire ax held high over his head. Jimmy planted himself solidly to the deck. He waited until he could count the buttons of the sailor's shirt, until he could see every fiber in the man's grass slippers.

Jimmy fired and the sailor was hurled back into the scuppers. Running up the ladder to the gunboat's bridge, Jimmy saw the light brighten there. A door had been opened. He stopped at the head of the companionway, watching.

Pete Gar's long arms came out of nowhere. Jimmy's revolver was thrown to one side. With a roar, Pete Gar threw his entire weight against Jimmy's chest. Jimmy staggered, almost thrown back down the ladder.

Jimmy turned to save himself the fall. He clattered down, hoping that Pete Gar had no weapon. Pete roared anew and gave instant pursuit. That was what Jimmy wanted.

Jimmy made as if to run across the gunboat deck, but before he could go ten steps, with Pete a pace behind him, he spun about and ducked under Pete's outstretched arms. Pete made an ineffectual stab at Jimmy's shoulder and then bellowed in pursuit back up the ladder.

The revolver lay on the deck where it had fallen. Jimmy scooped it up and wheeled. He fired without aiming, but it was impossible to miss. The triumph froze on Pete Gar's face. He toppled heavily backward to the deck below.

Jimmy knew that he would have to work fast. The fight on the *Shanung* couldn't last forever. He stared about him. Once more he saw the flickering light in the bow port of the steamer. That confirmed his deductions.

If Rockham had not been ashore, if he had not been with Lee Chang, if he was not on the gunboat, then he had only one place left. Rockham, naturally, must still be aboard the *Shanung*. It had seemed impossible at first, but then Jimmy knew that he had not thoroughly explored the vessel. He had spent almost all of his time on the top deck.

And what was that flickering light if not a signal? Otherwise it would have been a flashlight.

But first he had to make certain Virginia was there. He flung back the door to the bridge cabin.

From someplace within came the sound of fists hammering on wood. Jimmy leaped across the room and unfastened the small pantry door beyond. Virginia staggered into his arms, her face haggard, her lips trembling.

Jimmy smiled and gave her a tight hug. "Am I glad to see you, lady!" he cried.

"Ohhhhhh, Jimmy."

"Save it. Save it. I've got a hunch I know where Rockham

is. We've only got a minute or two before that fight stops over there. You stay here." He opened several drawers in the cabinet locker and pulled out an automatic which he thrust into her shaking hands.

"Stay here and shoot whoever comes in," he ordered.

Turning, he sprinted out across the bridge. He could hear the idling throb of the Diesel engines somewhere inside the gunboat. That was good. Of the three ships, the *Shanung*, the junk and the gunboat, only the last was ready for instant flight. His luck asserted itself again.

Already the fight was halting. Men were still killing each other in the darkness but the heat of the fray was gone. Now came the stalking, harsh, coldblooded murder, the lurking death behind each bitt and locker which might strike friend or foe. Jimmy knew that if he did not get out of there in the next couple of minutes, the fight would be completely over and his only avenue of escape blocked. The men would go back to the gunboat and he would be lost.

The dangerous, blood-greased deck of the steamer loomed over his head, but this was no time to falter. He had a hunch and he had to follow through. No Rockham ashore, nor on either gunboat or junk, and it stood to reason that the man could only be in one of those three places unless . . .

Unless he was still aboard the *Shanung*!

Up over the rail he went. A gigantic shadow sprang upright before him, steel in hand, already striking. Jimmy fired with a down chop.

The shadow melted back into the darkness with a shriek

of agony. Jimmy vaulted over the body and headed for the forward deck of the *Shanung*. Behind him came two Chinese, cat-footed and slow in their sureness of a kill. Jimmy did not see them as he plunged into a dim passageway of the fo'c's'le.

He tried the doors, savagely wrenching them open. He did not dare cry out. He had to trust to his sight and that, in this darkness, was something unreliable. His hunch told him that somewhere here he would find the man everyone wanted.

The maze of passages was quickly explored. From time to time Jimmy halted and listened, but he could hear nothing from the outside or the inside except the rap of guns and shouts on the deck.

Surely he could not be wrong, but wrong he must be. There were no other doors, no more passages. He had tried them all. He went down a steel ladder on one last hope. This was the paint shop. Light came faintly into it from the gunboat's deck alongside.

But, except for row on row of paint cans and the litter on the deck, the place was empty. Nothing here. He had failed and his hunch was wrong. He had to go back, the puzzle unsolved.

Rockham, he realized, must be down in Davy Jones' locker, one of the unidentified dead of the *Shanung*.

The realization and the hopelessness of it was a drug to his senses. Incautiously he stepped out into the passageway. The two Chinese who had followed him sprang forward.

Startled, Jimmy fired without aiming and missed. The two came on with a concerted yowl of triumph. Jimmy fired again, trying to turn and get away.

Halfway back into the paint shop, Jimmy tried again to bring down a Chinese. His slug twitched the man's sleeve, drew quick blood from the forearm.

The man's companion cried out a warning and threw himself through an open door, dragging his companion with him.

The suddenness of this move was something to distrust. This was not retreat. And it could only be one other thing. Jimmy realized in that second that he could not get back to the deck without passing that open door. They had him trapped!

He backed into the paint shop, gun ready, waiting for the Chinese to make the next move. Inwardly he raged at the time they took. A few more minutes and everything would be over for both himself and Virginia.

Waiting was hard for him. The seconds dragged into a minute and another minute followed, each fraction an hour long. He hoped the Chinese would think he had found another way out and venture into sight. If they did he would not take a fast shot again. He would aim carefully and well and make his slugs count. The cunning of the devils, waiting there in perfect safety, waiting for him to try to get out.

But, fortunately for Jimmy, the Chinese were also impatient. Their door creaked. Between the rap of shots outside Jimmy could hear them whispering. And then he heard a certain snicking sound which came from only one weapon.

A hand grenade!

They had pulled the pin and were ready to throw it into the paint shop.

If he had missed that sound he would have died where

he stood, but with that second's warning, he threw the door wide open and stepped behind it, shielding himself with its thick steel.

A ringing thump sounded on the floor not a foot beyond his barricade. He prayed that the fragments would miss him when they ricocheted about the room. It was an agony, waiting for the explosion to deafen him.

Suddenly the whole steamer seemed to rock under the impact. The door, blown back by the concussion, pinned Jimmy to the wall, almost smashing him in a steel sandwich.

Fulminate fumes were acrid in the shop. Paint was spilled and ran like blood sluggishly across the floor.

Jimmy marshaled his senses and stood up straight. The Chinese would come to see the damage and the corpse. And when they came . . .

The explosion had not even been noticed outside, so intent were the two crews upon their mutual murder. Other hand grenades had gone off before with horrible effect as the scuppers attested.

Bare feet whispered on the steel plates. A mutter of voices came to Jimmy. The two were coming. He tightened his hold on the automatic and stepped out from behind the door.

A face, blurred in the dimness, projected itself into the room. Jimmy fired, carefully aiming, at a range of two feet. The Chinese went down. The other, acting upon a fatal impulse, lunged forward, straight into the ribbon of flame the automatic stabbed at him.

The two sprawled across the jamb, fingers outstretched, weapons released. Jimmy started to cross them and get out.

He heard a faint shout. He whirled and looked back at the floor. Not until then did he notice that a hole had been blown through the plates by the hand grenade. Another faraway shout came again.

Quickly, his heart beating three times its usual speed, Jimmy leaned over the yawning black pit and stared down. He could hear the shout more clearly now. Someone was down there . . . somewhere . . . and it might be . . .

Jimmy lowered himself through the aperture and dropped to a deck he had not known existed. He struggled forward through dense blackness, his fingers exploring the way. Presently he encountered a steel square raised up out of this mysterious false deck.

And then he found a lock of the kind which automatically fastens itself upon closing. He pried it open and a cloud of smoke smote him in the face.

He knew then what had happened. This was a sort of false bow, tacked on to the regular bow. It must have been used by the *Shanung*'s owners as a safe for contraband. It was only accessible through the paint shop and then only by the removal of plates out of the deck. And here was a second hatch. Only a man who knew of its existence could have found it. Time after time it must have fooled revenue men.

And now it had been transformed into a living tomb from which there was no escape once a man went within and shut this hatch—thanks to that self-snapping lock.

Jimmy swore at himself for being a fool. He should have suspected something like this. He raised the hatch cover higher and smoke poured out again. For an instant he thought that the vessel must be on fire and then he saw a pot of oil and a rag—the light.

A man with a seamed and weary face stared blankly at him. Jimmy recognized the man from his pictures. It was George Harley Rockham.

"Come up," barked Jimmy.

Rockham was followed by two Chinese and a white man. They retreated a step from the sound of the fight and then at Jimmy's orders came on. Jimmy led the group back through the paint shop to the deck.

"Get over the side to that gunboat," ordered Jimmy.

"Who are you?" demanded Rockham in a thin voice.

"Jimmy Vance of the *Oriental Press*. Snap into it, will you?"

Rockham blinked and then made haste to bridge the gap between the two vessels. The other white man and the two Chinese scrambled after him. Jimmy, nervously covering their retreat, faced the deck of the *Shanung*.

A shaft of light came from the bridge of the gunboat and lay yellow across the *Shanung*'s slippery plates. Through it weaved two men. One was dressed in a scarlet jacket, the other was clothed all in black.

The latter drew Jimmy's attention. "Cheng!" he gasped. "What the hell is that blackguard doing here?"

Cheng and Lee Chang struggled together, leader against leader, Cheng fighting for the upraised blade of the jade knife. Jimmy stepped forward, intending to do something, anything. But before he could get there, the knife swept down.

Jimmy expected to see the sleek Cheng collapse. But instead

the scarlet jacket shivered. The knife protruded from the pirate's throat.

With a yell, Cheng sprang back. His black gown was torn, his round face was bleeding. He ran swiftly toward the gunboat.

Suddenly he saw Jimmy. He stopped with a gasp, too surprised to do anything for a second. Jimmy reached forward with a swift motion. Cheng was dragged off his feet.

The gun in Jimmy's hand came down and rapped a smart blow upon the black hair of the ambassador-at-large.

Then, dragging Cheng, Jimmy went over the gunboat rail and back to the bridge. He thrust the inert Cheng into Rockham's unsteady hands.

"Take care of this guy," ordered Jimmy.

Jimmy raced back to the rail. A fire ax lay on the deck, dropped by the man he had shot. Jimmy picked it up and hacked through the hawsers.

Shots came from the *Shanung*'s bridge, splintering the deck about Jimmy. But he did not pause until he had severed the two lines. Then the gunboat, carried by the swell, drifted out away from the *Shanung*, leaving the dying mutter of the fight.

Jimmy went below, toward the sound of the idling Diesels. He threw back the bulkhead door.

Burt stood against the far side of the shining engine room. With him was the man called Joe. They stared at Jimmy's gun and then carefully elevated their hands.

Jimmy eyed them coldly. "I ought to shoot you devils now, but I won't. I'll leave you for the Execution Park in Shanghai."

"How the devil . . . ?" began Burt, jolted out of his calm.

Jimmy noticed the fireroom door and saw that a hose locker stood open beside it. "Back into that," he snapped.

Burt backed. Joe, glancing nervously about, followed suit. They crammed themselves into the small interior. Jimmy advanced and slammed the door in their faces, locking it from the outside.

That done, Jimmy threw the Diesels into half speed ahead. He ran up through the hatch to the bridge to catch the wheel before the drive of the engines could put the gunboat back against the *Shanung*. But one of the sailors he had released with Rockham was already there.

"Steer out to sea," said Jimmy. "Steer anyplace as long as it's away from Bias Bay."

The yellow man nodded and steered away from the carnage aboard the *Shanung*.

CHAPTER ELEVEN

HOMEWARD BOUND

WHEN Jimmy returned to the big bridge cabin, he found a very silent circle awaiting him. Cheng was stretched out on the floor, his suave face very marred, his mouth open.

Everyone looked at Jimmy expectantly. Virginia, smiling and tired, moved to his side.

George Harley Rockham, a man about fifty, looked very starved, very haggard. He reached out and shook Jimmy's hand. His kindly eyes glowed his thanks.

The other white man advanced and took the hand. "I'm Johnson," he said, "Mr. Rockham's secretary."

"Pleased to meet you," said Jimmy. "How did all this happen?"

"It was my fault," Johnson replied. "When this gunboat first approached the *Shanung*, it flew a Chinese Navy flag. We were up on the bridge with the captain and when the gunboat got close, it gave orders for us to heave to. The captain understood instantly that something was wrong. Mr. Rockham was all for staying on the scene, so . . ."

Rockham smiled. "So you laid me out and packed me off to that lazarette alongside of gallons of paint. Two Chinese members of the crew were already there. If it hadn't been for the carpenter's quarters and the water spigot there and the cases of sea biscuit, we'd have died. We couldn't open the hatch with anything. It locked from the outside. And when we first heard the plane, we thought it was pirates again and we didn't make a sound. We thought this last fight was between sailors and pirates. We didn't know. Thank God you rescued us, boy."

Cheng was coming to, moving feebly. Jimmy knelt beside him and shook him fully awake. Cheng looked about him, dazedly.

Rockham looked at Cheng and started. "What the devil is this, Cheng?"

Cheng avoided Rockham's eyes.

"Speak up," snapped Rockham. "You were at the bottom of this. Talk!"

Cheng, at Jimmy's none-too-kind-urgings, talked. "I was hired by Manchukuo to get you and kill you. I fitted out this old gunboat and attacked the *Shanung*, intending to . . ."

"Go on," snapped Jimmy.

"Intending to make it look like pirates did it. But we couldn't find you, Rockham. Where were you?"

"Never mind that," said Rockham.

"Manchukuo knew that if you disappeared your interests would go to the devil. You had the oil monopoly up there. Manchukuo didn't want you to have it. They needed their fields back again. In another day we could have done it, but . . ."

"You'll probably hang," said Jimmy, cheerfully. "Look here, is there a radio aboard this tub?"

"Yes," moaned Cheng.

"This is colossal," cried Jimmy. "The government of

Manchukuo engineered this to get back oil concessions they couldn't buy! Where *is* that radio?"

Jimmy went swiftly out to the deck, saw the radio shack and turned in. He tested the switches, found juice in the lines and seated himself at the key.

Virginia, after he had gone, smiled at Rockham. "He did it all," she said, softly.

"He's a fine lad, Virginia," agreed Rockham. "A fine lad. He's got the pressure and the energy I need."

"You'll have it," said Virginia. "I think . . . I think I'm going to marry him." And she went out, following Jimmy into the radio shack.

When Jimmy had contacted the Shanghai station of the *Oriental Press,* his key finger rattled like castanets gone mad. He composed the story as he sent it.

"Bias Bay," clattered Jimmy. "George Harley Rockham was found a few minutes ago by a reporter of the *Oriental Press.* Having been held captive aboard the *Shanung* for several days, he was discovered . . ."

Virginia was at his side, her arm around his shoulders. Jimmy looked up, still sending, and smiled happily. With his left hand he drew her down to him and found her red lips very soft.

The operator at the Shanghai station snapped, "What the merry hell is this, anyway. Is Jimmy nuts?"

For the phones were crackling, "I love you! I love you!" And from the crash of the dots and dashes, the Shanghai operator knew that Jimmy meant it.

STORY PREVIEW

NOW that you've just ventured through one of the captivating tales in the Stories from the Golden Age collection by L. Ron Hubbard, turn the page and enjoy a preview of *Mister Tidwell, Gunner.* Join Mister Tidwell, who's pressed into British naval service to teach twelve-year old midshipmen of Lord Nelson's fleet. But this Oxford-educated academic soon finds himself thrust into the heat of battle with Napoleon's forces, alone and without support.

MISTER TIDWELL, GUNNER

MISTER TIDWELL watched them go. Harvey and Sloan. Twelve years old, future officers, two of an uncontrollable band of twenty-four who harassed officers and men and Mister Tidwell without mercy.

Especially Mister Tidwell. He was their schoolmaster.

The crackbrained idea which sent young men of twelve to sea, fostered in the dim past by King Charles, who thought his navy needed officers trained from infancy, had only been capped by another king's thought that these urchins should have the benefits of schooling at the hands of a trained master.

Mister Tidwell, along with several score of well-meaning professors, had long suffered the effects of those laws.

The small pay and the arduous life offered little attraction to any man of the day, much less a learned gentleman, and so His Majesty had been forced to conceive a stratagem which was nothing more than literary press ganging.

Two years before Mister Tidwell had written a paper. A mild, well worded paper, which dealt with the tax system. For that he had been sent to sea. And here he was, standing in the *Swiftsure*'s scuppers, watching battle approach, knowing that he was even now late for the cockpit.

Marines swarmed up the ratlines, white crossbelts shimmering, muskets clenched, faces strained as they took their posts in the crosstrees. Mister Tidwell envied those Marines. Their sole duty consisted of taking pot shots at Marines in the rigging of the French ships, and what if they did die? They at least stayed out in the sun and air.

The long and short of Mister Tidwell's aversion to answering that call to quarters was blood.

A horizontal plume of smoke rapped out from the Frenchman's bow chasers. Round shot smashed solidly into the rail. Splinters sang like shrapnel. Two sailors clutched their lacerated faces and leaned sickly against their guns. One of them looked at the maw of the hatch from whence came a stream of powder monkeys bearing their leathern buckets. He looked away again and strove to staunch the flow of blood with his white cotton shirt. No, that gunner certainly did not want to go below to the hospital.

The Frenchman was a quarter of a mile away, swinging into position for a broadside. On the *Swiftsure,* drums still rolled and trumpets blared, filling Mister Tidwell with uneasiness.

Gun captains blew on their matches. A twenty-four pounder spurted flame from muzzle and touchhole, leaped up and slammed back on the deck, splintering a wooden wheel. The shot sang through the Frenchman's rigging.

The broadside smashed out, enveloping the entire enemy ship with smoke. Sails and spars rained on the *Swiftsure's* deck. A Marine came down like a shot tropical bird, hitting the planks solidly to roll over on his face. An officer leaned over him for a moment, hand pressed against the crimsoning crossbelts, and then jerked his thumb toward the rail. The Marine was thrown over the side.

Lucky, thought Mister Tidwell. The man hadn't lived to see the cockpit in action.

A hand fell on Tidwell's shoulder. A petty officer, face contorted with excitement and anger, shook the gray coat and sent Mister Tidwell hurtling toward the hatch.

A midshipman, holding a musket bigger than he was, paused in his ascent up a ratline long enough to grin. Mister Tidwell reproved the boy with a glance and then went below.

No one paid any attention to him on the second gun deck. The cannon had begun to fire, bucking out of line, filling the place with choking fumes. Mister Tidwell paused for a moment, reluctant to go below again. He saw the sweating torsos of the gunners through the dim welter of round shot, flying splinters, gashed beams and exploding guns.

He sighed, and then shrugging his small shoulders inside his gray frock coat, he adjusted his eye glasses and went down another ladder to the third gun deck.

The stream of black powder monkeys and their black cargoes choked the passageway for a moment. Mister Tidwell stood aside to let them by. Powder was strewn all over the planking. One match would finish the ship. It was ever thus.

Mister Tidwell went aft, ducking his head to avoid the beams. A tall man was forced to take to his hands and knees through this passageway. The cockpit was ahead.

A great lantern filled with sputtering candles burned against the beams. The midshipmen slept here when things were peaceful. Now the midshipmen's chests had been drawn together to make a low table. A piece of tarpaulin, already black with blood, was spread over the surface.

The surgeon, a tall, gaunt impassive gentleman, stood over a small stove heating his saws and knives and soldering irons. His assistants were placing buckets all about the improvised table, making ready for the men soon to come.

This was Mister Tidwell's battle station. Here he was no longer schoolmaster to the midshipmen, he was part of the surgeon's machine.

To find out more about *Mister Tidwell, Gunner* and how you can obtain your copy, go to www.goldenagestories.com.

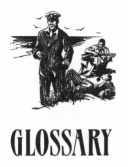

GLOSSARY

STORIES FROM THE GOLDEN AGE *reflect the words and expressions used in the 1930s and 1940s, adding unique flavor and authenticity to the tales. While a character's speech may often reflect regional origins, it also can convey attitudes common in the day. So that readers can better grasp such cultural and historical terms, uncommon words or expressions of the era, the following glossary has been provided.*

---

bearder: one who boldly confronts or challenges (someone formidable).

Bias Bay: body of water off the coast of China, fifty miles northeast of Hong Kong, and notorious as a base of operations for Chinese pirates.

bitt: a vertical post, usually one of a pair, set on the deck of a ship and used for securing cables, lines for towing, etc.

blackguard: a man who behaves in a dishonorable or contemptible way.

bow chasers: a pair of long guns mounted forward in the bow of a sailing warship to fire directly ahead; used when chasing an enemy to shoot away her sails and rigging.

bow eyes: eyes painted on either side of the bow of a ship. The term comes from the ancient custom of painting eyes on the bow so that the ship could see where she was going.

bridge wings: narrow walkways extending outward from both sides of a pilothouse to the full width of a ship.

broadside: all the guns that can be fired from one side of a warship or their simultaneous fire in naval warfare.

Bund: the word *bund* means an embankment and "the Bund" refers to a particular stretch of embanked riverfront along the Huangpu River in Shanghai that is lined with dozens of historical buildings. The Bund lies north of the old walled city of Shanghai. This was initially a British settlement; later the British and American settlements were combined into the International Settlement. A building boom at the end of the nineteenth century and beginning of the twentieth century led to the Bund becoming a major financial hub of East Asia.

Canton: city and port in the southern part of China, northwest of Hong Kong.

Chinwangtao: port city of northwest China on the Bo Hai Sea, an inlet of the Yellow Sea, 186 miles (300 km) east of Beijing. It was formerly a treaty port where foreign trade was allowed.

cleats: pieces of metal or wood having projecting arms or ends on which a rope can be wound or secured.

cockpit: a cabin on the lower deck of a man-o'-war where the wounded in battle were tended.

Cossack jacket: *cherkeska;* a military coatlike garment with silver cartridges lined across the chest. The cartridges are a reminder of the times when the Cossacks were armed with muzzle-loading guns. At that time, each cartridge contained enough gunpowder for one shot. When breech-loading weapons came into use, the holders were retained as part of the costume.

crate: an airplane.

crosstrees: a pair of horizontal rods attached to a sailing ship's mast to spread the rigging, especially at the head of a topmast.

davits: any of various cranelike devices, used singly or in pairs, for supporting, raising and lowering boats, anchors and cargo over a hatchway or side of a ship.

Davy Jones' locker: the ocean's bottom, especially when regarded as the grave of all who perish at sea.

dead to rights: in the very act of committing a crime, offense or mistake; red-handed.

dodger: a canvas or wood screen to provide protection from ocean spray on a ship.

dyed-in-the-wool: thoroughgoing; out-and-out.

fills: copy used primarily to fill extra space in a column or page of a newspaper or periodical, especially a brief item of fact as from a reference book.

five-spot: a five-dollar bill.

fo'c's'le: forecastle; the upper deck of a sailing ship, forward of the foremast.

forecastle head: the extreme fore part of the upper deck of a sailing ship, forward of the foremast.

foredeck: the part of a ship's deck between the bridge and the forecastle (the upper deck of a sailing ship, forward of the foremast).

founder: to sink below the surface of the water.

fulminate: fulminate of mercury; a gray crystalline powder that when dry explodes under percussion or heat and is used in detonators and as a high explosive.

gaff: a pole rising aft from a mast to support the top of a sail.

galleon: a large three-masted sailing ship, usually with two or more decks; used mainly by the Spanish from the fifteenth to eighteenth centuries for war and commerce.

gangway: a narrow, movable platform or ramp forming a bridge by which to board or leave a ship.

gats: pistols.

G-men: government men; agents of the Federal Bureau of Investigation.

gun captain: a petty officer in command of a gun crew on a ship.

gunwale: the upper edge of the side of a boat. Originally a gunwale was a platform where guns were mounted, and was designed to accommodate the additional stresses imposed by the artillery being used.

hawsers: cables or ropes used in mooring or towing ships.

heave to: to bring a ship to a stop.

horse pistol: a single-shot .58-caliber handgun created in 1805, resembling a short-barreled rifle. The gun was designed to be carried in a holster on the side of a horse, and was known as a hard-hitting and powerful weapon.

Huangpu: a long river in China flowing through Shanghai. It is a major navigational route, lined with wharves, warehouses and industrial plants, and provides access to Shanghai for oceangoing vessels.

hull down: sufficiently far away, or below the horizon, that the hull is invisible.

junk: a seagoing ship with a traditional Chinese design and used primarily in Chinese waters. Junks have square sails spread by battens (long flat wooden strips for strengthening a sail), a high stern and usually a flat bottom.

key: a hand-operated device used to transmit Morse code messages.

Kowloon: a city of southeastern China on Kowloon Peninsula opposite Hong Kong Island.

lazarette: a small storeroom within the hull of a ship, especially one at the extreme stern.

Manchukuo: a former state of eastern Asia in Manchuria and eastern Inner Mongolia. In 1932 it was established as a puppet state (a country that is nominally independent, but in reality is under the control of another power) after the Japanese invaded Manchuria in 1931. It was returned to the Chinese government in 1945.

Mex: Mexican peso; in 1732 it was introduced as a trade coin with China and was so popular that China became one of its principal consumers. Mexico minted and exported pesos to China until 1949. It was issued as both coins and paper money.

midshipman: a student naval officer educated principally at sea.

military brushes: a pair of matched hairbrushes having no handles, especially for men.

morning coat: a man's single-breasted coat. The front parts usually meet at one button in the middle, and gently curve away into a pair of tails behind. The coat can be gray or black and is usually worn with striped trousers. The name derives from the fact that a common form of morning exercise for gentlemen in the nineteenth century was horseback riding, and because of this it was regarded as a more casual way of dress.

newshawk: a newspaper reporter, especially one who is energetic and aggressive.

painter: a rope, usually at the bow, for fastening a boat to a ship, stake, etc.

powder monkeys: boys employed on warships to carry gunpowder from the magazine to the guns.

press ganging: forcing (a person) into military or naval service.

quarter: mercy or indulgence, especially as shown in sparing a life and accepting the surrender of a vanquished enemy.

ratline: a small rope fastened horizontally between the shrouds in the rigging of a sailing ship to form a rung of a ladder for the crew going aloft.

sampan: any of various small boats of the Far East, as one propelled by a single oar over the stern and provided with a roofing of mats.

Scheherazade: the female narrator of *The Arabian Nights*, who during one thousand and one adventurous nights saved her life by entertaining her husband, the king, with stories.

sculling oar: a single oar that is moved from side to side, at the stern of a boat, to propel it forward.

scuppers: openings in the side of a ship at deck level that allow water to run off.

seven great sea oaths: an abundance of profanities or swearwords. The seven great seas is in reference to the many seas of the world.

Seventh Hell: in Chinese mythology, hell is depicted as an underground maze with eighteen different levels and the Seventh Hell refers to the seventh lowest level.

Shanghai: city of eastern China at the mouth of the Yangtze River, and the largest city in the country. Shanghai was opened to foreign trade by treaty in 1842 and quickly prospered. France, Great Britain and the United States all held large concessions (rights to use land granted by a government) in the city until the early twentieth century.

Shantung: a peninsula in east China extending into the Yellow Sea.

spars: strong poles, especially those used as masts to support the sails on ships.

spat: a piece of cloth or leather covering the ankle and part of the shoe, and fastened on the side of the shoe. Spats are worn by men.

SS: steamship.

steerageway: the minimum rate of motion sufficient to make a ship or boat respond to movements of the rudder.

sweeps: long, heavy oars.

.38 Colt: a .38-caliber automatic handgun manufactured by the Colt Firearms Company, founded in 1847 by Samuel Colt (1814–1862) who revolutionized the firearms industry with his inventions.

thole: a holder attached to the gunwale of a boat that holds the oar in place, and acts as a fulcrum for rowing.

tiffin: a meal at midday; a luncheon.

transom: transom seat; a kind of bench seat, usually with a locker or drawers underneath.

waist: the central part of a ship.

Who's Who: a reference book or reference serial providing brief biographical information about well-known people who are still living.

Yangtze: the longest river in Asia and the third longest in the world, after the Nile in Africa and the Amazon in South America.

Yellow Sea: an arm of the Pacific Ocean between the Chinese mainland and the Korean Peninsula. It connects with the East China Sea to the south.

L. Ron Hubbard
in the Golden Age
of Pulp Fiction

*In writing an adventure story
a writer has to know that he is adventuring
for a lot of people who cannot.
The writer has to take them here and there
about the globe and show them
excitement and love and realism.
As long as that writer is living the part of an
adventurer when he is hammering
the keys, he is succeeding with his story.*

*Adventuring is a state of mind.
If you adventure through life, you have a
good chance to be a success on paper.*

*Adventure doesn't mean globe-trotting,
exactly, and it doesn't mean great deeds.
Adventuring is like art.
You have to live it to make it real.*

—L. RON HUBBARD

L. Ron Hubbard
and American
Pulp Fiction

ORN March 13, 1911, L. Ron Hubbard lived a life at
Bleast as expansive as the stories with which he enthralled
a hundred million readers through a fifty-year career.

Originally hailing from Tilden, Nebraska, he spent his
formative years in a classically rugged Montana, replete with
the cowpunchers, lawmen and desperadoes who would later
people his Wild West adventures. And lest anyone imagine
those adventures were drawn from vicarious experience, he
was not only breaking broncs at a tender age, he was also
among the few whites ever admitted into Blackfoot society
as a bona fide blood brother. While if only to round out an
otherwise rough and tumble youth, his mother was that rarity
of her time—a thoroughly educated woman—who introduced
her son to the classics of Occidental literature even before his
seventh birthday.

But as any dedicated L. Ron Hubbard reader will attest, his
world extended far beyond Montana. In point of fact, and as the
son of a United States naval officer, by the age of eighteen he
had traveled over a quarter of a million miles. Included therein
were three Pacific crossings to a then still mysterious Asia, where
he ran with the likes of Her British Majesty's agent-in-place

L. Ron Hubbard, left, at Congressional Airport, Washington, DC, 1931, with members of George Washington University flying club.

for North China, and the last in the line of Royal Magicians from the court of Kublai Khan. For the record, L. Ron Hubbard was also among the first Westerners to gain admittance to forbidden Tibetan monasteries below Manchuria, and his photographs of China's Great Wall long graced American geography texts.

Upon his return to the United States and a hasty completion of his interrupted high school education, the young Ron Hubbard entered George Washington University. There, as fans of his aerial adventures may have heard, he earned his wings as a pioneering barnstormer at the dawn of American aviation. He also earned a place in free-flight record books for the longest sustained flight above Chicago. Moreover, as a roving reporter for *Sportsman Pilot* (featuring his first professionally penned articles), he further helped inspire a generation of pilots who would take America to world airpower.

Immediately beyond his sophomore year, Ron embarked on the first of his famed ethnological expeditions, initially to then untrammeled Caribbean shores (descriptions of which would later fill a whole series of West Indies mystery-thrillers). That the Puerto Rican interior would also figure into the future of Ron Hubbard stories was likewise no accident. For in addition to cultural studies of the island, a 1932–33

LRH expedition is rightly remembered as conducting the first complete mineralogical survey of a Puerto Rico under United States jurisdiction.

There was many another adventure along this vein: As a lifetime member of the famed Explorers Club, L. Ron Hubbard charted North Pacific waters with the first shipboard radio direction finder, and so pioneered a long-range navigation system universally employed until the late twentieth century. While not to put too fine an edge on it, he also held a rare Master Mariner's license to pilot any vessel, of any tonnage in any ocean.

Yet lest we stray too far afield, there is an LRH note at this juncture in his saga, and it reads in part:

"I started out writing for the pulps, writing the best I knew, writing for every mag on the stands, slanting as well as I could."

To which one might add: His earliest submissions date from the summer of 1934, and included tales drawn from true-to-life Asian adventures, with characters roughly modeled on British/American intelligence operatives he had known in Shanghai. His early Westerns were similarly peppered with details drawn from personal

Capt. L. Ron Hubbard in Ketchikan, Alaska, 1940, on his Alaskan Radio Experimental Expedition, the first of three voyages conducted under the Explorers Club flag.

experience. Although therein lay a first hard lesson from the often cruel world of the pulps. His first Westerns were soundly rejected as lacking the authenticity of a Max Brand yarn (a particularly frustrating comment given L. Ron Hubbard's Westerns came straight from his Montana homeland, while Max Brand was a mediocre New York poet named Frederick Schiller Faust, who turned out implausible six-shooter tales from the terrace of an Italian villa).

Nevertheless, and needless to say, L. Ron Hubbard persevered and soon earned a reputation as among the most publishable names in pulp fiction, with a ninety percent placement rate of first-draft manuscripts. He was also among the most prolific, averaging between seventy and a hundred thousand words a month. Hence the rumors that L. Ron Hubbard had redesigned a typewriter for faster keyboard action and pounded out manuscripts on a continuous roll of butcher paper to save the precious seconds it took to insert a single sheet of paper into manual typewriters of the day.

That all L. Ron Hubbard stories did not run beneath said byline is yet another aspect of pulp fiction lore. That is, as publishers periodically rejected manuscripts from top-drawer authors if only to avoid paying top dollar, L. Ron Hubbard and company just as frequently replied with submissions under various pseudonyms. In Ron's case, the list

A MAN OF MANY NAMES

Between 1934 and 1950, L. Ron Hubbard authored more than fifteen million words of fiction in more than two hundred classic publications. To supply his fans and editors with stories across an array of genres and pulp titles, he adopted fifteen pseudonyms in addition to his already renowned L. Ron Hubbard byline.

Winchester Remington Colt
Lt. Jonathan Daly
Capt. Charles Gordon
Capt. L. Ron Hubbard
Bernard Hubbel
Michael Keith
Rene Lafayette
Legionnaire 148
Legionnaire 14830
Ken Martin
Scott Morgan
Lt. Scott Morgan
Kurt von Rachen
Barry Randolph
Capt. Humbert Reynolds

included: Rene Lafayette, Captain Charles Gordon, Lt. Scott Morgan and the notorious Kurt von Rachen—supposedly on the lam for a murder rap, while hammering out two-fisted prose in Argentina. The point: While L. Ron Hubbard as Ken Martin spun stories of Southeast Asian intrigue, LRH as Barry Randolph authored tales of

L. Ron Hubbard, circa 1930, at the outset of a literary career that would finally span half a century.

romance on the Western range—which, stretching between a dozen genres is how he came to stand among the two hundred elite authors providing close to a million tales through the glory days of American Pulp Fiction.

In evidence of exactly that, by 1936 L. Ron Hubbard was literally leading pulp fiction's elite as president of New York's American Fiction Guild. Members included a veritable pulp hall of fame: Lester "Doc Savage" Dent, Walter "The Shadow" Gibson, and the legendary Dashiell Hammett—to cite but a few.

Also in evidence of just where L. Ron Hubbard stood within his first two years on the American pulp circuit: By the spring of 1937, he was ensconced in Hollywood, adopting a Caribbean thriller for Columbia Pictures, remembered today as *The Secret of Treasure Island.* Comprising fifteen thirty-minute episodes, the L. Ron Hubbard screenplay led to the most profitable matinée serial in Hollywood history. In accord with Hollywood culture, he was thereafter continually called

The 1937 Secret of Treasure Island, *a fifteen-episode serial adapted for the screen by L. Ron Hubbard from his novel,* Murder at Pirate ́ Castle.

upon to rewrite/doctor scripts—most famously for long-time friend and fellow adventurer Clark Gable.

In the interim—and herein lies another distinctive chapter of the L. Ron Hubbard story—he continually worked to open Pulp Kingdom gates to up-and-coming authors. Or, for that matter, anyone who wished to write. It was a fairly unconventional stance, as markets were already thin and competition razor sharp. But the fact remains, it was an L. Ron Hubbard hallmark that he vehemently lobbied on behalf of young authors—regularly supplying instructional articles to trade journals, guest-lecturing to short story classes at George Washington University and Harvard, and even founding his own creative writing competition. It was established in 1940, dubbed the Golden Pen, and guaranteed winners both New York representation and publication in *Argosy*.

But it was John W. Campbell Jr.'s *Astounding Science Fiction* that finally proved the most memorable LRH vehicle. While every fan of L. Ron Hubbard's galactic epics undoubtedly knows the story, it nonetheless bears repeating: By late 1938, the pulp publishing magnate of Street & Smith was determined to revamp *Astounding Science Fiction* for broader readership. In particular, senior editorial director F. Orlin Tremaine called for stories with a stronger *human element*. When acting editor John W. Campbell balked, preferring his spaceship-driven tales,

Tremaine enlisted Hubbard. Hubbard, in turn, replied with the genre's first truly *character-driven* works, wherein heroes are pitted not against bug-eyed monsters but the mystery and majesty of deep space itself—and thus was launched the Golden Age of Science Fiction.

The names alone are enough to quicken the pulse of any science fiction aficionado, including LRH friend and protégé, Robert Heinlein, Isaac Asimov, A. E. van Vogt and Ray Bradbury. Moreover, when coupled with LRH stories of fantasy, we further come to what's rightly been described as the foundation of every modern tale of horror: L. Ron Hubbard's immortal *Fear*. It was rightly proclaimed by Stephen King as one of the very few works to genuinely warrant that overworked term "classic"—as in: *"This is a classic tale of creeping, surreal menace and horror. . . . This is one of the really, really good ones."*

L. Ron Hubbard, 1948, among fellow science fiction luminaries at the World Science Fiction Convention in Toronto.

To accommodate the greater body of L. Ron Hubbard fantasies, Street & Smith inaugurated *Unknown*—a classic pulp if there ever was one, and wherein readers were soon thrilling to the likes of *Typewriter in the Sky* and *Slaves of Sleep* of which Frederik Pohl would declare: *"There are bits and pieces from Ron's work that became part of the language in ways that very few other writers managed."*

And, indeed, at J. W. Campbell Jr.'s insistence, Ron was regularly drawing on themes from the Arabian Nights and so introducing readers to a world of genies, jinn, Aladdin and Sinbad—all of which, of course, continue to float through cultural mythology to this day.

At least as influential in terms of post-apocalypse stories was L. Ron Hubbard's 1940 *Final Blackout*. Generally acclaimed as the finest anti-war novel of the decade and among the ten best works of the genre ever authored—here, too, was a tale that would live on in ways few other writers

imagined. Hence, the later Robert Heinlein verdict: "Final Blackout *is as perfect a piece of science fiction as has ever been written."*

Like many another who both lived and wrote American pulp adventure, the war proved a tragic end to Ron's sojourn in the pulps. He served with distinction in four theaters and was highly decorated for commanding corvettes in the North Pacific. He was also grievously wounded in combat, lost many a close friend and colleague and thus resolved to say farewell to pulp fiction and devote himself to what it had supported these many years—namely, his serious research.

Portland, Oregon, 1943; L. Ron Hubbard captain of the US Navy subchaser PC 815.

But in no way was the LRH literary saga at an end, for as he wrote some thirty years later, in 1980:

"Recently there came a period when I had little to do. This was novel in a life so crammed with busy years, and I decided to amuse myself by writing a novel that was pure science fiction."

That work was *Battlefield Earth: A Saga of the Year 3000.* It was an immediate *New York Times* bestseller and, in fact, the first international science fiction blockbuster in decades. It was not, however, L. Ron Hubbard's magnum opus, as that distinction is generally reserved for his next and final work: The 1.2 million word *Mission Earth.*

> **Final Blackout**
> *is as perfect a piece of science fiction as has ever been written.*
>
> —Robert Heinlein

How he managed those 1.2 million words in just over twelve months is yet another piece of the L. Ron Hubbard legend. But the fact remains, he did indeed author a ten-volume *dekalogy* that lives in publishing history for the fact that each and every volume of the series was also a *New York Times* bestseller.

Moreover, as subsequent generations discovered L. Ron Hubbard through republished works and novelizations of his screenplays, the mere fact of his name on a cover signaled an international bestseller. . . . Until, to date, sales of his works exceed hundreds of millions, and he otherwise remains among the most enduring and widely read authors in literary history. Although as a final word on the tales of L. Ron Hubbard, perhaps it's enough to simply reiterate what editors told readers in the glory days of American Pulp Fiction:

He writes the way he does, brothers, because he's been there, seen it and done it!

THE STORIES FROM THE GOLDEN AGE

Your ticket to adventure starts here with the Stories from
the Golden Age collection by master storyteller L. Ron Hubbard.
These gripping tales are set in a kaleidoscope of exotic locales and brim
with fascinating characters, including some of the
most vile villains, dangerous dames and brazen heroes
you'll ever get to meet.

The entire collection of over one hundred and fifty stories is being
released in a series of eighty books and audiobooks.
For an up-to-date listing of available titles,
go to www.goldenagestories.com.

AIR ADVENTURE

Arctic Wings	*Man-Killers of the Air*
The Battling Pilot	*On Blazing Wings*
Boomerang Bomber	*Red Death Over China*
The Crate Killer	*Sabotage in the Sky*
The Dive Bomber	*Sky Birds Dare!*
Forbidden Gold	*The Sky-Crasher*
Hurtling Wings	*Trouble on His Wings*
The Lieutenant Takes the Sky	*Wings Over Ethiopia*

FAR-FLUNG ADVENTURE

SEA ADVENTURE

TALES FROM THE ORIENT

MYSTERY

FANTASY

SCIENCE FICTION

WESTERN

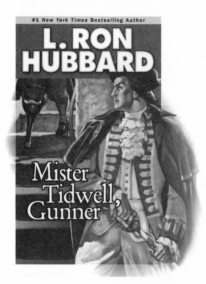